The Cabin at the End of the Train

A Story About Pursuing Dreams

MICHAEL V. IVANOV

ISBN-13: 979-8-9853041-3-8

If you would like to have Michael speak at your corporate event,
school, retreat, church, or any other event, please visit Michael's
website below

Special discounts are available on quantity purchases by corporations,
associations, and others. For details, contact the publisher at the web
address below.

www.SPEAKLIFE365.com

This book is dedicated to my readers. I hope it inspires you to pursue your dreams, the time is now! Thank you from the bottom of my heart. I hope you enjoy this one too, dear friends.

-Michael

Other books by Michael V. Ivanov

The Mount of Olives:
11 Declarations to an Extraordinary Life

The Traveler's Secret:
Ancient Proverbs for Better Living

The Servant With One Talent:
Five Success Principles from the Greatest Parable
Ever Told

Contents

One

"Sometimes the things we run from are the very things we should be moving towards"

I checked my phone for the tenth time that morning and shoved it back into my jeans pocket. Precisely thirty minutes until boarding began.

Just enough time to grab a coffee and get to the station.

I was drumming my fingers against my knees but tried to remain still when I noticed Makenzie glance at them.

"Can you stop by the Black Rock?" I asked, looking over at her. "I'll run in and grab a coffee to take with me on the train. We should be good on time."

"I don't want you to be late, babe," she cautioned as she merged the car onto the freeway. "They aren't going to wait for one passenger."

"I'll be fine." I placed my hand on her shoulder and gently squeezed. Her hair was a mess, and the clothes she sleepily threw on before we rushed out of the door gave her that careless Walmart shopper appearance everyone jokes about. She wore her new puffy winter coat over old pajamas and long winter boots. I thought about snapping a photo to tease her later—but decided against it as she was doing me a huge favor that morning.

Besides, she *looked* like a mess but at least had an excuse—it was early. I *was* a mess, and it didn't matter how I was dressed or how much I joked around; internally, I was anything but put together.

"Unless you want to run in and grab it for me while I wait in the car?" I slapped her arm and forced a smile, hoping to hide my anxiousness.

"Yes, absolutely," she said. "I'll just walk in looking like a hobo like this is how I normally dress."

I chuckled at her sarcasm, but then my mind shot back to my trip, and I glanced at the clock on her dash. *5:01 AM.* I still had twenty-nine minutes.

I'll definitely have time to get a coffee . . . I should have time.

"Morning, Mike!"

I heard Levi's cheerful voice before I spotted my favorite barista's head pop up from behind the counter. I let the door gently close behind me to keep the bells on the wreath from bouncing against the glass door.

Levi has been there to greet and serve me on hundreds of early mornings over the years. I make sure he gets a copy of every book I write. I figure the least I can do is satisfy his curiosity with the finished product of all that typing he sees me do. With every project, I'm in there month after month, painstakingly turning words into sentences, sentences into paragraphs, and paragraphs into chapters until a new book is born. I get cabin fever when I write at my home desk for long periods, so the coffee shop has become my second office.

The smell of roasted beans instantly filled my nostrils, and I exhaled, relaxing my shoulders. A strong cup of coffee or a stiff drink was about the only thing that could calm me and bring me into the present moment. Especially lately—it seemed like even my short morning prayers and walks weren't helping anymore.

Luckily there was also writing. When I was working on a book, I could disappear into another world. But when I wasn't, I couldn't escape my own without the help of a drink or some other distraction. I rarely felt entirely at ease. In my mind, there was no downtime. I was always planning, thinking, and overthinking.

Maybe I wasn't exercising, drinking enough water, or giving myself enough time before I rushed into my lengthy to-do list every morning? Who knows . . . I was out of ideas.

I believed this is just how it is when you put yourself out there and pursue a big dream.

When you commit to doing something out of the ordinary, it's not comfortable. You leave yourself vulnerable to failure and criticism. You're constantly doing things that stretch your mind, test your patience, and rattle your confidence. I figured the constant unease was just part of the process and meant that I was headed in the right direction.

I wanted not just to entertain people but to inspire them. I wanted to inspire readers like my favorite author, Og Mandino, had inspired me. I wanted to be a great writer. And I wanted to be a motivational speaker because Og Mandino was a motivational speaker.

I was depressed and purposeless when I found one of his books in a used book cart at the local library. I was a twenty-five-year-old kid then, living for the weekend— hating Mondays when I would have to trudge back to my cubicle at work, and cherishing Fridays when I routinely snuck out early to beat traffic and start my weekend. That's when I could finally forget about work for two short days.

I don't know what made me pick up his book, *A Better Way to Live*. The tattered paperback only cost me a dollar and changed my life forever—a heck of a deal for a total transformation. That's when I knew I wanted to become a writer and speaker, even though I was petrified of public speaking. In fact, I'd been so scared that I'd dropped my speech class in college after freezing up during a three-minute presentation and forgetting the remainder of my ill-prepared speech. With a beet-red face and burning ears, I slunk out of the classroom and never returned.

And still, after reading Og's book, I knew that was what I wanted to do—speak and write . . . I had to. I was drawn to it with certainty I still can't explain.

An older man in overalls and shin-high rubber boots walked into the shop and stood behind me as I waited for Levi to finish serving another customer. I glanced back, and our eyes met, so I nodded and quickly turned my attention back to the counter.

"It's a good day, isn't it?" I heard him say behind me.

"What . . . oh, yes." I turned my head over my shoulder to answer without looking at him.

Crap, I shouldn't have looked back.

I wasn't sure if he was talking about the fact that it was Christmas Eve, or maybe he was personally having a good start to his day and wanted to tell me about it, but I didn't care to hear it either way. I knew how to dodge small talk with strangers, and I was getting good at it. Keep your answers short and avoid eye contact;

eventually, they get the hint.

The man in overalls did because he left me alone, and I was back into my own thoughts.

I was chasing something. Sometimes I forgot what it was, but I knew I was chasing something. I wanted to do great things with my life. I wanted to leave a legacy and make a mark on the world. I dreaded being a "nobody." Everybody craves recognition, even if they don't admit it. None of us want to exist without being seen, heard, or remembered.

And I could finally see a way to achieving that—if I could realize this new dream that was born in me, I could become somebody. I knew that if I was long-gone some years from now, and some poor lost soul found one of my books, and it changed his life . . . it would have all been worth it. If someone found an old recording of one of my speeches and it helped to transform their beliefs positively, I would have impacted the world. What better reward was there than being credited for changing someone's life? I couldn't think of any. That's a job from which I wouldn't want to retire. So that's what I needed to do.

I was well on my way, too. I already saw things I once only visualized come to pass. Years ago, when I was still sitting in my cubicle at the little printing company I worked for, I'd sketch myself standing on stages before large audiences. Now, I had already delivered speeches to audiences of several thousand people. I drew book covers with my name on them, imagining myself being a published author. Now, I'd already written and published several books.

And yet even after authoring my books and speaking on those stages, my confident, optimistic, inspiring future self still felt so far away. I'd thought surely when I hit those milestones; I would have it made. I would embrace the extraordinary version of Michael Victor Ivanov and never look back. And then I would help others do the same. I would never be a "nobody" again. People would know my name. People would credit me for their transformations.

But oddly enough, the opposite happened. The more progress I made, my fears evolved, and the more insecurities arose. The bigger the stages I spoke on, the more I felt like an imposter. The more books I sold, the more I felt corralled by people's expectations and opinions of me; I feared readers who thought highly of my work would discover the real me and be disappointed. I wasn't so sure if I wanted to be credited for anything anymore.

For some mysterious reason, I was beginning to feel like to achieve everything I desired; I had to find and flip some secret switch in my mind—finally allowing myself to accept that I was worthy and that I belonged with the best. Only I couldn't find the switch.

I felt insecure, unqualified—and like I knew less about myself than I did before.

Life seemed much simpler in the past when I was living for the weekend . . . That's probably why so many people stay complacent—at least it's comfortable and safe, even if you are rotting away in a cubicle.

Perhaps that was why I didn't sleep. I told people I was a light sleeper, but that was an understatement and a half-truth. A car passing by my house or leaves rustling in the wind by my bedroom window would jar me awake, and I'd spend the next few hours in torment.

I'd lie awake, tossing and turning as I wondered if I'd become everything I wanted to become or if I was just wasting the years chasing some fantasy while my wife and family patiently waited for me to come back to reality. Maybe they were hoping I would eventually get serious about my finances, job security, and future. Had I gone past the point of no return?

Maybe I should just go back to my old boss, beg for a job, establish a safe career, and start a family before it's too late. Maybe if I quit all of this and settle, I can finally get some sleep. Would that be such a bad trade?

Over the years, the more I learned about the business of speaking and book-selling, the more I understood how far I still had to go. I wasn't famous, and I didn't have an agent. There were no shortcuts for an unknown like me.

Despite my progress and some incredible opportunities that had come my way thus far, I had a lot to accomplish before I could consider writing and speaking a successful career. My speaking engagements weren't consistent, nor were the book royalties guaranteed each month.

To add to the pressure, everyone around me seemed to be moving on in life. Children were being born, beer guts were growing, and my once wild-and-free friends settled down. One morning I discovered a single gray hair on my beard and was depressed for the entire day. And yet, I continued hammering away at my laptop, writing books and contacting speaker agents daily, putting all my chips on the table and betting on my dream.

The nights were gruelingly long if I had an upcoming speech. I rehearsed daily for hours, and when night came, I stared at the ceiling again, feeling stupid and like a phony, wondering how I landed that speaking engagement in the first place. *Is this my last opportunity? What if I bore the audience to death? What if my mind goes blank, and I make a fool of myself as I did in college? Do I even belong on the same stage as the other speakers?*

Surely I was the only speaker on the conference agenda lying wide awake, questioning myself. Did that mean I wasn't following my true purpose? *If this is my calling, why the hell is it so damn hard!?* It sure felt like I was headed in the wrong direction when the night was the darkest.

I understood that sometimes the things we run from are

the things we should be moving towards. But how could I successfully inspire people if I was still so distressed before every speech and believed there were probably *thousands* of speakers more naturally talented and comfortable than I? Would that feeling ever go away? How could I write books about principles for better living when I struggled to live by them?

The doubt only made me more restless.

But I couldn't stop obsessing. I wanted success more than anything in the world, and I thought if I ever took a break from working on my business, I would become complacent and lose momentum. So I kept calculating, estimating, hoping, wishing, praying, constantly ruminating about the future, and missing the little moments happening all around me. Incredible family and friends surrounded me, and yet most of the time, I couldn't stay present when we were together.

How can I enjoy life if I'm not yet where I want to be? I often asked myself.

Happiness would come later. I hadn't sold a million books yet as I had dreamed of doing. I hadn't booked my schedule solid with speaking engagements like I had promised myself I would do by now.

Yet I was so ready to be done with feeling less qualified than everyone else doing what I was doing. I hated feeling like an imposter. For once, I just wanted eight hours of sleep before a speaking engagement. For once, I wanted to be okay with someone not liking me, or my books, or my speech. By now, I should have defeated those fears.

What the heck am I doing wrong?

I was sure that once I accomplished my goals, I would stop doubting myself, my mind would be at peace, and I would be content. Then, and only then, I could relax and enjoy those lazy evenings and holidays with family without my mind wandering into the future. Then I would be successful. I knew I wasn't there yet, and now I wasn't so sure I would ever get there.

"How's the famous author?" Levi smiled as he handed me my usual—a medium breve with six shots. I didn't have to order; Levi always started on my drink when he saw me pull into the parking lot.

"Ready for Christmas, Mike?"

"Yep, yep," I replied and looked behind me, hoping the man in overalls didn't overhear the *author* bit.

"How about you, man? Get your shopping done?" I quickly asked.

"You know it!"

I was especially anxious this Christmas Eve morning. I would take the train alone and not spend Christmas with my wife or family. By design, it would be just me and my thoughts for four days. I needed time to think. I had no business in the Midwest when I bought the ticket from Vancouver, Washington, to Chicago Union Station a few days prior. I planned to ride the train there and back and hoped that the isolated journey would somehow be enough time to get my thoughts and my life in order, or at least gain a little more clarity and find some peace. God, I needed it.

***

I leaned over and pecked Makenzie on the cheek.

"Thank you for understanding. I know it's Christmas, but the last thing I need is to be around people. No one besides myself can help me figure this thing out . . . and I have *got* to get my mind in order. I might not get a chance to retake a trip like this for a while."

"Oh, my goodness, of course!" she exclaimed. "I just wish I could somehow help, but I know this is something you need to do—we'll just make Christmas super big next year." My most loyal supporter smiled big, and my guilt about missing Christmas only increased. I couldn't handle this year; who knows how much worse I'd be by next year.

I threw my backpack over my shoulder and grabbed my duffle bag from the back seat. Then I headed through the parking lot into Vancouver Station. As I passed near the train, I was startled by the sudden ear-deafening hiss from the brakes releasing pressure and thought it was odd there was no one around on the platform. This place was usually bustling in the early morning.

Two

"Your eyes are the window through which the soul sees the world"

I glanced at my phone and saw a couple of missed texts. *Damn,* I should have been checking for Amtrak notifications. I missed the updated departure time after I purchased the tickets. When the girl at the counter checked my reservation, she rushed me out the door and radioed ahead to get me on the train, just in time. Now I knew why the station was empty—everyone had already boarded. I was the last one on the train.

My coffee stop—an attempt at holding on to some sense of familiarity this anxious morning—had almost cost me the trip.

I headed up the aisle, moving through one full car after the other, squeezing around passengers already lined up at the restrooms, and stopping to let a mother pull her two wrestling twins off the floor so I could sneak through. I continued through the bar car, an observation car, and up the narrow hallways through the sleeper cars near the front of the train. I eventually found my room, a tight but cozy little "roomette" along the left side of the train, roughly four feet wide between the window and the door to the hall where I stood. The large window spanned nearly the entire room length, and the two bench seats facing each other could be unfolded into a bed. I pulled open the black-out drapes covering the thick glass; I didn't want to miss the views as we rolled out of Vancouver and into the Columbia River Gorge.

I shed my coat, shoved my duffle bag under the seat next to my backpack, and headed for the last car as I felt the train lurch forward. Something about the last car at the end of the train had caught my eye, and I wanted to investigate.

I opened the heavy wood door and saw that the interior of the last car didn't match the design of the rest of the train, which was expectedly modern with USB ports and reading lights built into each of the large, cushioned seats. All the cars had standard Amtrak-issue teal carpets and matching drapes with white plastic paneling just like my roomette. However, the car at the end of the train looked to be from another era, perhaps from a much older train.

Its paneled interior was dark, elegantly carved, and polished wood. The dim Edison bulbs above reflected from the long narrow mirror on the ceiling where the rounded panel walls met, giving the car a warm ambient glow. I looked up at my reflection in the ceiling mirror and tamed my beard. That's when I noticed the thick bottle green carpet under my feet. To my surprise, as antique as the cabin looked, there wasn't a single stain or worn patch, as if it was only recently installed and not something that had been in use since the early 1900s as I imagined.

What is this?

The car was divided into two cabins. The first where I stood was the bar. Its illuminated shelves were designed to be stacked with liquor, running up to the ceiling on either side of a large mirror. But these shelves were empty. Six tall stools bolted to the floor surrounded the bar top; their dark green velvet seats matched the carpet and had no signs of wear, as if the stools, like the carpet, had never been used. There wasn't a speck of dust on the bar or the empty shelves.

A narrow door with a small oval window at eye level separated the two cabins. With its little curtain pulled to the side, I could peek into the last cabin as I approached it. I glanced behind me, wondering if I'd get in trouble wandering back there.

Maybe this car is being transported to a museum? It certainly looked much too elegant and antique to be a part of the ordinary passenger train headed to Chicago. I pushed through the door with one hand, still clutching my coffee. Inside the last cabin were two identical classic couches along the walls facing each other and several oak chairs, cushioned and stitched with green velvet, like the bar stools.

Thick crystal cigar trays and two dimly lit vintage lamps stood on each matching mahogany end table. I wished Makenzie was with me. She would have thought this car was romantic; she loved anything to do with early 1900s fashion and design. I felt like I was in an old movie and expected to see travelers wearing three-piece suits, pocket watches, top hats, and smoking cigars. I was definitely out of place in my worn sneakers, my favorite baseball cap I bought from a street vendor in Boston, a hoodie, and jeans.

I walked to the back of the cabin, pulled the fancy tasseled curtains aside to peek out the window, and spotted the gold knob. I looked behind me again to see if anyone was around and pulled on it.

To my surprise, it wasn't locked, and I was suddenly standing on the back balcony of the speeding train with nothing but a steel railing between me and the tracks. Cold winter air mixed with blowing snow kicked up from the train instantly enveloped me, and I looked back at the warm glow from the cabin.

Am I on the freaking Orient Express?

I gently pushed the door so that it would appear closed from the inside but didn't shut it in case anyone else came into the car after me. I would freeze to death if I somehow got locked out. Pulling my sweater tighter around my neck and holding onto the railing, I watched Vancouver disappear behind the bend as the train thundered alongside the Columbia River. I spotted the headlights of a few cars on Highway 14 as we rode parallel with it until it curved and began its climb, vanishing into the mountains. It was the morning of Christmas Eve, and people had finally settled in for a few days after the chaotic weeks leading up to the holidays. Besides those few cars, the roads were empty.

I guessed the other passengers on the train were last-minute holiday travelers, likely avoiding driving in the snow. The news reported that many mountain passes in Washington, Idaho, and Montana had been closed due to the heavy snowfall.

How awesome would it be if I had this cabin all to myself for the rest of the trip? Between these views and the cabin, I could use some serious alone time in such incredible luxury.

The sky lightened to gray as the sun rose somewhere high above the snow clouds. After a few minutes, it became unbearable to stand out on the balcony in my thin hoodie and t-shirt. I might as well have been shirtless. I carefully walked through and out of the last car, making sure no one saw me step out, and headed for my roomette.

***

I sipped my coffee and ate a sandwich with my feet kicked up against the opposite seat in my room, watching the Columbia River Gorge unfold outside of my window. I had driven through the Gorge at least a thousand times in my life—it was one of the most beautiful places in all of America, and we Pacific Northwesterners were lucky to have it in our backyard. But I had never seen it from the train, and with the snow blanketed over the rock formations, cliffs, and endless mountains of evergreens; I couldn't help but admire its beauty anew. I had grown accustomed to it and certainly took it for granted after all these years. As the jagged cliffs towered overhead, disappearing high into the early morning fog, I just sat and took long deep breaths.

This is what I needed—being alone and soaking up the beauty of nature.

It was striking to suddenly realize that simply looking at something so peaceful and serene put my mind into a state of peace. It was as if my soul had dried up, and I was reviving it by merely placing my eyes on something that, for once, did not trigger anxiety, worry, or insecurity. I had often heard the saying, "the eyes are the window into the soul," but I had never heard anyone talk about the eyes being the window through which the soul experiences the world.

Lately, I have been receiving one rejection email after another. Receiving more no's than yesses is a necessary part of the process when growing in just about any business or career or chasing a dream, especially when trying to break into a competitive industry. But looking through those emails first thing in the morning wasn't doing me any favors.

Whether it was an event I was pitching, a speaker agency, or a bookseller, I was constantly reminded that I wasn't good enough. At least that's how I was interpreting it. Day after day, month after month, year after year, I saw or heard the dreaded "unfortunately" in each wordy email or phone call.

"*Unfortunately,* you were not selected."

"*Unfortunately,* we are no longer accepting new talent."

"*Unfortunately,* we are not interested in representing your book at this time."

I had heard them all, yet I kept sending proposals and bugging people.

I also didn't help myself by constantly scrolling through social media and seeing the success of authors and speakers who were where I wanted to be. It reminded me I was falling behind even more. *I'm not doing enough,* I often thought—so I'd double down and send more inquiries, but the rejections certainly took their toll on me.

In rare times like this, when I took a lengthy break from the noise and the hustle, the world seemed a bit more normal; I felt in control of my life and didn't feel so much like a failure. I don't know why I didn't remember to take more breaks; simply focusing my eyes and attention on things that gave me peace, hope, and joy made me feel whole again.

I inhaled again and released slowly, letting my breath out through my nose as the train passed along the river, entering and exiting one tunnel after another. I couldn't believe how much the physical body responded to thought and thought alone. It hit me now that I was breathing shallow and losing sleep for what seemed like ages just because I was always in my head, ruminating over something.

I reached under my seat and pulled my journal out of my backpack. Flipping through years of notes, observations, dreams, and plans scribbled and dated on the early pages of the old notebook until I found a blank page. Perhaps these weren't new ideas, but they were new to me.

The eyes aren't just windows into the soul; they are also the window through which the soul sees the world. How can the soul be at peace if presented with only negativity and failure? And how can the soul experience negativity and disappointment if it meditates on all those good, authentic, and positive things, despite the chaos? This is one of those things one can only discover by allowing themselves the space to think.

I couldn't afford to go this long again without giving my soul some time away from the chaos to flourish.

I spent the rest of the day in my roomette until evening, leaving only to grab lunch, use the restroom, and stretch my legs when the train stopped in Pasco and Spokane. I had brought a few books with me and planned on reading later that afternoon in the observation car but found every seat occupied. I decided that later I would grab a drink and read in the unique cabin at the end of the train if it was still unlocked.

I hoped it would be.

It was starting to get dark, and snow fell again when I headed for the bar. We would be in Sandpoint within the hour, and I wanted to get a drink before the rush of people getting on and off. I paid for my double Old Fashioned and carefully headed for the last car with Og Mandino's *"A Better Way to Live"* tucked into my armpit. I had read the book dozens of times and still carried it in my backpack wherever I went. Its purple paperback cover was torn and discolored but miraculously intact. The very same one I had purchased for a dollar so many years ago. I hoped rereading it might bring back some of those powerful feelings of possibility it once ignited in me. I needed it.

It was one of the rare books where Og wrote about his personal life story instead of his typical inspirational fiction.

Og described how he flew a B-24 Liberator, a heavy bomber plane in World War II, and co-piloted missions with actor James Stewart. When he returned from the war, Og became an unsuccessful insurance salesman, then an alcoholic, causing his wife and child to leave him. On a wintry night in Cleveland, he spotted a pistol in the window of a pawn shop and decided to buy it to kill himself, but the pawn shop was closed. Instead, he took refuge from the cold in the public library, and there, to avoid getting kicked out, he read books by authors like Napoleon Hill, W. Clement Stone, and many other inspirational classics.

Books change lives. Thousands of successful people throughout history have attributed their success to the books they read, and although I was far from where I wanted to be, I can say without a doubt that reading transformed my life, too.

This book, Og's personal story, first ignited my dream years ago to write and speak. I sat in my work cubicle and read the book repeatedly, and something stirred in me. Sometimes it brought me to tears. As if God himself was nudging me, daring me to dream, to believe that I was capable of doing so much more than writing boring lines of code for a small printing company that valued its profits over its employees. But the idea of leaving the safety of a consistent paycheck seemed so far out of reach.

At the time, I had been begging for answers, searching for purpose, and wishing for something better in my life. My answers came when I spotted that title in the library, possibly in the same way Og had done with the books that changed his life in that library where he found refuge. The same way that I dream my books will one day be found by that lost soul, searching for a better way to live.

I was happy to see no passengers around as I approached the antique car and looked behind me again to ensure no one further up in the train was watching me. I pulled on the handle. Still unlocked! I slipped into the car, passed by the old bar, and gently closed the divider door between the two cabins behind me just as I felt the train slow for the Sandpoint station.

Soon the train lurched forward and was leaving Sandpoint behind in the wintry dusk when I heard the door to the car open. I quietly set my whisky on the end table, clutching the open book I was reading and approached the divider door to peek through the oval window. A bearded old man with a cane held onto the bar table as he curiously examined it, just like I had that morning.

He wore a black windbreaker, wet from the flakes melting on his shoulders, and a trucker's hat with gold stitching on the front—I recognized the cap immediately. He was a World War II veteran.

Three

"You will feel afraid and unqualified"

I guessed the old man would eventually wander back out of the car, so I tip-toed across the spongy green carpet back to the couch, but just as I took my seat and got comfortable again, the divider door swung open.

"How's it going?" I said, trying to sound as friendly as possible but also like I belonged there. More of a "Can I help you?" than a "Hello."

"Oh!" He appeared startled, clearly expecting the car to be empty. "What an extraordinary car," he said. "I took a minute to admire it; I hope I'm not bothering you."

"Absolutely not," I replied. "I just discovered it myself earlier today. It reminds me of a movie I recently saw about the Orient Express. The only crappy thing about it is the bar is empty. I had to balance my drink all the way down here. didn't spill a drop!" I smiled and held up my half-empty glass.

He returned my smile, gripping both hands on the handle of his cane. "Yeah, that's the good stuff; you don't want to spill any of that."

I pointed to the curtained door at the back end of the cabin, "There's a balcony too, but I wouldn't suggest going out there. It's pretty cold."

He ignored me and released the grip on his cane with one hand to reach for the couch directly across from me. I laid my book down and jumped up to help, but he had already taken a seat. "Oh, I'm ok," he groaned. "I can still take care of myself."

I laughed nervously and sat back down across from him. I never wholly relaxed around old people. I respected them dearly—that was the way I was raised. So I never wanted to talk too much, slouch, or say something that might make me look foolish or like a punk know-it-all. These were people with a lifetime of wisdom, so I knew to keep my tongue on a short leash. For Russians, seniority is everything. My dad would always say to my brothers and me, "Never disrespect someone older than you, even if it's only a year older."

We learned that lesson very quickly in our household. Out of eight boys and five girls in the family, I am child number six. If I ever talked back to my older brothers or sisters, they'd smack me, and then Dad would give me an extra smack for good measure, even if I thought I was justified.

I was shocked when I first saw how American kids talk to their teachers. I couldn't believe they were getting away with mouthing off to an adult. Then I was stupid enough to try it, too. My 5th-grade teacher was Mr. Kotsubas, one of the kindest teachers I'd ever had, but in trying to impress some friends, I gave him a hard time one day in class. My friends laughed, but when I got home, my brother warned me that Mr. Kotsubas had called, and I thought my life was over.

To my surprise, my dad never said a word. He didn't need to. The look he gave me when I walked into the kitchen later that evening spoke more to me than any words or belt whipping ever would. That lesson stayed with me for the rest of my life. Publicly humiliating my dad, someone I deeply respected and loved, was enough of a punishment for me. I felt terrible for weeks.

I glanced at the old man and then back down at my book, unsure if I should introduce myself or pretend to be reading. His eyes wandered from the carpet to the thick blue curtains to the mirror on the ceiling. "Magnificent, just like a train I once rode as a boy."

"Oh yeah?" I folded the corner of a page to mark my spot and closed the book. "It's definitely from a different time. I wouldn't mind riding back here all the way to Chicago."

The old man continued to look around. I expected him to elaborate on that childhood memory, but he didn't. I looked at the lettering embroidered on his hat and wondered if it would be appropriate to ask him where he served. My grandfather, who I was named after, fought for the Red Army in World War II. He was captured on the outskirts of Leningrad, the city known as Saint Petersburg today. He was one of those Russian teens who were sent into battle to attack the Nazi encirclement without a rifle. The Russian army was short of weapons at the time, so he was given a pack of five bullets and ordered to charge with the hope of finding a rifle somewhere along the way. For nine hundred days, the Nazis had Leningrad surrounded to starve the three million civilians and soldiers trapped inside the city. However, in the end, after nearly a million dead Russians, they still failed to capture the city. Today we know it as the "Siege of Leningrad."

But my grandfather was not lucky enough to be a part of the eventual victory; he was captured after a night of dodging snipers in a muddy field—and then spent four years in the Dachau concentration camp. Eventually, American soldiers liberated his camp and freed him.

Storytime around the dinner table was my favorite when I was a kid. Our after-dinner entertainment was learning about "the old days" from my parents. My brothers and sisters and I would huddle around the dinner table, listening to my dad tell us about growing up with a communist government and all the stories Grandpa had told him about the war and the concentration camps. We were glued to him, even during the stories we had heard a thousand times. My dad always made them enjoyable each time. Sometimes he'd be in the middle of a story and tear up, staring at the table for what felt like an eternity, and then stir his teaspoon slowly and get back to the story. He is the best storyteller I know.

I complained about it then, but boy was I glad now there was no TV in the house when we were growing up. I still share those tales in my speeches because nothing drives a life principle home like a good story.

I looked at the old man again but stopped myself, deciding not to ask about his hat. He peered at me, my whiskey glass, and my book.

"Where are you headed, young man?" he asked in a deep, strained voice.

I thought of making something up so I wouldn't have to explain my first-world problems to a veteran who had undoubtedly experienced real troubles.

"I'm actually taking a roundtrip to Chicago and back." I blurted. "Just . . . just needed to get away from everything for a bit and thought this would give me some time to think."

The old man raised his brows. "On Christmas?"

I nodded, slightly embarrassed. I hoped he wouldn't pry further. He'd probably think I was just another modern-day sissy, worried about my little "problems."

He kept staring at me, leaning forward on his cane with both arms. I stirred my drink uncomfortably and took a sip. Finally, he asked, still not breaking his stare, "Is this because you don't know where you're headed? Or because you don't know if you can handle what is required of you to make it there?"

I gazed at my sneakers through the golden brown liquid in my glass, taken aback by how precisely the old man had guessed my dilemma. You have to give credit to that generation; if they are curious about something, they don't hesitate to ask. There's no tip-toeing around people's privacy or comfort, or feelings.

"I guess the latter, sir," I replied. "I definitely know where I'm headed. I just don't know if I can get there . . . or if I should get there . . . or if I even belong there."

"Then you must be working on something important . . . important enough to miss Christmas with your family." He tapped his fingers against his cane and watched for my reaction.

"Yes, sir, you could say it is important. At least to me, it is."

The old man just nodded.

"I'm a motivational speaker, and I'm also a writer. But I'm not just trying to entertain people like so many motivational speakers do; I want to change lives . . . like my favorite author." I held up Og's book.

"The thing is, I'm already well on my way, too. It . . . it's not like I'm just starting, you know?"

There was no reaction from the old man. He just waited for me to continue. So to avoid more silence, I kept talking.

"Since I started a couple of years ago, I've had some incredible opportunities to speak on stages that were only a dream in the past." I clicked my fingernails against the whiskey glass and then laughed nervously, hoping he somehow understood.

"The problem is I'm still scared. I'm afraid every time. I feel like an imposter and hate feeling that way.

"I thought it would go away by now, especially since I've already done it many times. So now I often wonder if I am supposed to be doing it. If maybe I'm not cut out for it and if maybe I just went for this dream only because I wanted to do something cool."

I sipped my whiskey and glanced at the old man. The liquor must have already been having its effect on me because here I was rambling to this man about insecurities I rarely even mention to Makenzie.

"I don't know," I shrugged. "Maybe it's not what I should be doing."

He started to smile but instantly straightened his wrinkled face again and waited a moment to see if I was done before he spoke, perhaps not wanting to make me feel worse about my self-doubt.

"First of all, I can tell you for certain you are on the right track. Luke-warm people don't feel pressured because their boss and TV Guide make their schedule for them."

"Hmm, that's true," I smirked.

"And second of all, give yourself a damn break," he chuckled, holding up his palm. "I'm not here to judge. There's no need to justify yourself in front of an old man."

I was embarrassed, realizing I'd broken my rule of blabbing too much. After another minute of silence, the old man sat up a little straighter.

"Have you heard a speaker say they can get up onto a stage and 'speak about anything for hours without being nervous?'"

I nodded and exhaled, glad he was moving on with the conversation. "Yes, sir, I have, and I'm jealous of that kind of confidence."

"Well, you shouldn't be." His bushy white brows scrunched together. "Someone who gets up in front of a group of people and Yakety-yaks without having anything important to say usually is not a person worth listening to." He lifted his hat by the bill to adjust it, revealing his bald, bruised scalp for a moment.

"I've seen these so-called speakers, even preachers, who hold the audience prisoner for sixty minutes, trying to come up with things to say on the fly to fill their time . . . repeating themselves over and over again. 'I don't need to prepare. It's all in my head,' they say, and then go on and on, never saying much of anything."

He stroked his beard before continuing. "You can talk about nothing when you're having coffee with a friend but don't be casual when you are given an opportunity in front of an audience."

I sighed. "Very true, sir. I certainly take it seriously, maybe too seriously. That's probably why it haunts me so much."

He raised his brows, stretching the wrinkled skin around his deep-set eyes, and pointed a crooked finger at me, "If you are careless for one hour in a conversation, you've wasted one hour. But you have wasted how many hours of life with an audience of a thousand people?" He waited for me to catch on.

"One thousand hours," I answered.

"Smart man," he replied.

I was pleasantly surprised to see that he understood the weightiness and art of public speaking, as it was something I very much held in high regard. What most people see as "natural talent" or "gifting" on stage is actually the result of a ton of behind-the-scenes effort and preparation by a speaker, at least a good one.

We sat silently for a few moments, gently rocked by the speeding train as it made its way through the Rocky Mountains. I gazed at their faint outlines through the window over the old man's shoulder before he spoke again.

"Sometimes it took Winston Churchill several hours to write a few sentences into his speeches."

I had read a lot about Churchill, perhaps the greatest orator of his time, and listened to his recordings. I knew how hard he worked to blend the right words with the best examples and how he searched for the most potent metaphors until he was satisfied. I thought about him when I wrote my speeches.

The old man continued, "He studied and knew the power of words."

"Hell!" he chuckled, "Even Hitler obsessed about his speeches!"

"Yep!" I laughed. "I haven't studied Hitler's speeches. I'm not ready to start a war, but clearly, the man knew what he was doing, even if it was used for evil."

I thought about Churchill and how his mind blanked

during one of his first attempts at delivering a speech and how he sat back down without saying a word. I was happy when I learned this because that's precisely what happened to me in my college speaking class, and I'd never felt more stupid. Except Churchill froze up in front of an audience of thousands, and I was in front of just fifteen students. If he had a hill to overcome, I had a mountain. At least that's the way I saw it back then.

After that botched speech in college, I swore I would *never* speak again in front of a group of people. Little did I know where my life would take me. Things really do come full circle. Despite how far I had to go, I had come a long way.

The old vet wiped his nose with a handkerchief, folded it, and then shoved it back into his khaki pants.

"When doing something extraordinary, you will feel afraid and unqualified. You will feel like that most of the time. The key is to have the courage to do it anyway. There can be no courage without fear."

I smiled and saw my opportunity to ask him about his service, "Well, I can't compare my fears to what you must have experienced in the war, but that certainly is a better perspective than I have on fear!"

He shrugged. "We all have our obstacles; it doesn't help to compare unless you compare to gain perspective." He looked out over his shoulder to the shadowy outlines of the Rockies.

This time *I* waited. I hoped more than anything that he would keep talking. I learned a long time ago that the wisest thing you can do in the presence of old people is to shut up and listen. They are a fountain of stories, experiences, and perspectives. And they are hilarious. I don't know if I've ever spoken to an old person who didn't make me laugh. They could care less about what you think of them or their honest observations, and I loved that. We need more of that in today's tip-toeing around people's feelings and walking on eggshells world.

I was sitting across a World War II veteran, a living legend of the greatest generation; it was an extra special moment for me. I've watched thousands of hours of war documentaries. I studied all the battles, from tank skirmishes in the mud to dogfights in the sky. I practically considered myself an expert war historian. So much so that I could determine the accuracy and budget of any war movie I watched by the weapons and machinery used in the film by the Axis or the Allies.

The old man was sharp, wise, and seemed to understand me instantly. Earlier, I wanted nothing more than to be left alone—now, I was very much enjoying his company.

He shut his eyes, stuck his chin forward as if he were taking a big gulp, and then spoke, this time in a low, quiet voice.

"There is a kind of fear that I hope to God you never experience, young man . . . the kind that makes the hair on your neck stand and spreads through you until you are just about paralyzed. The kind of fear that'll make your blood ice over."

He paused for an entire minute with his eyes still closed. I held my breath.

"One day, we got an order; our mission was to beat the Germans out of a little village and destroy a railroad nearby to stop their supply runs. Well . . . sometime late in the afternoon, our tanks rolled up to the village . . . if you could call it that, it hardly resembled a village. I was driving the lead tank, and when I peeked through the hatch, I saw the flames from burning homes, barns, and a church, bursting a hundred feet into the air, and everything smelled like burning flesh. I . . ." he let out a sigh, "I saw a child screaming at the feet of her mother's corpse. The Germans had hung her mother from a tree. We couldn't stop to take the little girl with us because the Germans were hitting us with everything they had . . ." I heard his voice break, and he paused for a moment before he finished his thought.

"So we drove on through. I never found out what happened to her. And I'll never forget her. You don't feel God in a moment like that. You only feel as if you are entering the gates of hell, and that is the loneliest I have ever felt before. When you see what human beings are capable of doing to one another . . ." He exhaled and dropped his shoulders as he opened his eyes. Just reliving the moment seemed to take the energy right out of him.

I held my breath and stupidly nodded as if I understood what he was saying. I didn't. I couldn't even imagine it.

"But as I said, there can be no courage without fear." He said after a long pause. "We were just boys . . . afraid, and unqualified, but we did what we were asked to do even though we were scared as hell."

The old man's willingness to share such a horrific experience surprised me; it wasn't common for veterans to speak about what they witnessed at war. Most returned home and buried those memories for good.

After a few minutes of silence, I reached across the carpet and stretched out my hand. "Thank you for your service, sir. My name is Michael; I appreciate you giving me a little perspective tonight."

"Carl, Carl Talbot," he answered and shook my hand.

"It's nice to meet you, Carl; can I buy you a drink?

"Oh hell . . . why not?" Carl shrugged.

Four

"You will be pulled in all directions"

I ordered two Old Fashioneds and dodged several passengers on my way to the last car. I pushed through the door with my hip and immediately spotted a chubby man in a blue suit, maroon tie, and thick glasses sitting in my seat across from Carl. *Crap,* I thought. *He's probably kicking us out.*

Carl took the glass with both hands and nodded at the tense man in my seat. "This is Austin, a salesman from Chicago."

"How's it going, Austin?" I said and glanced at my book next to him. "Oh, this must be your seat." He said in a soft apologetic voice and grabbed his black leather briefcase. He hurriedly scooted down the couch. I set my glass down on the end table and got comfortable in my seat.

At first, because of his thinning blonde hair and double

chin, I guessed he was about forty, but when I heard his soft voice and noticed his smooth, red cheeks, I figured he couldn't have been more than a few years past his teens.

"I thought you were here to kick us out of the Orient Express," I said and extended my hand. He adjusted his glasses with the tips of his fingers, brushed them on his suit, and shook my hand firmly.

"Ha, no. I actually just wanted to find a seat away from everyone else. I was surprised to find this unique car here. I wish the bar were open!"

"It is a few cars up," I said, "They make excellent Old Fashioneds . . . if you're old enough." I teased and pointed in the direction of the door.

"I know," he laughed nervously, "It's the baby face. I'm twenty-two. I'll go get a drink here in a minute."

Carl turned his attention to the kid. "Austin, tell me this . . . what's a salesman doing riding a train across the country on Christmas Eve dressed like he just got out of a meeting? You selling last-minute wreaths?"

We all laughed.

"No, though I might have had better luck with that!" His eyes darted between Carl and me. He set his briefcase on the carpet next to his feet and finally seemed to relax in his seat. "I guess you could say I was desperate . . . doing more hoping than planning. I sell roofs. I came to the Pacific Northwest because I heard it rains a lot here, thought I might catch a break with all the moss and wetness. But I hadn't sold a single roof install after three weeks."

He adjusted his thick glasses again and stared at his scuffed black dress shoes. "Now I'm heading home to my wife and nine-month-old. Just wish I wasn't coming back empty-handed."

I instantly felt sorry for the kid. He seemed like one of those open-book guys with no hidden agenda. Someone you could be comfortable around within minutes of being in the same room. Guys like Austin didn't one-up your stories or size you up before deciding if you were worth their time and attention. I liked him immediately. I couldn't stand to see people try and fail, especially open, genuine kids like him.

So many people lived sedentary, mediocre lives. Sometimes I wished God could reward those out there at least trying to make something of themselves. I knew that's not how it worked, but one could wish.

Would it be so hard to let the poor kid get a few sales? I complained to God in my head.

Austin gave me the impression he was a kid who hadn't had too many wins in his young life. He seemed defeated and unsure of himself.

"Well, keep persisting, man," I exclaimed. "It's a tough time of the year to be selling. Most folks were racking up credit card debt buying Christmas presents the last few weeks, so I can't imagine there were too many people eager to sign up for a shingle remodel and commit to more monthly payments. I'm sure it'll be worth your trip if you come back in the spring."

"Yeah, I knew it was a bad time to come down. I just heard a few other fellas from my company had some luck, and I'm new to the business, so I thought I'd give it a try while the rest of the sales guys were taking it easy for the holidays. Now I see why they were," he sighed.

Carl seemed to be addressing Austin, but he was looking at me as he replied. "You know, when you spend too much time watching other people's success, you forget to steer your own."

He looked at Austin. "Do you remember when you were learning how to drive? How you learn to keep your eyes on the road because the car goes where your eyes go?"

The kid nodded.

"In life, people will pull you to the left or the right, but rarely to where you want to go. You'll likely end up in a ditch if you're not keeping the wheel on course."

I smiled. *I should probably be taking notes—Carl has gold here.* He seemed to have answers for everything. I loved it.

"Everyone has opportunities and shortcuts to offer . . ." The old vet took a sip from his glass and then pointed two fingers directly at Austin's eyes, "You've got to learn to keep your eyes on the road and not let every promise of riches pull you this way or that way.

"Frank Sinatra once sang, 'I've lived a life that's full, I traveled each and every highway, and more, much more . . . I did it my way!' If you want to succeed, you've got to find *your way.*"

Now he looked at me, and I knew he was addressing both of us. "Life will tempt you at every turn. It will present you with an obstacle here and an opportunity there. It will play on your fears and throw your insecurities in your face just to see if you will settle and give up on your dreams. Don't fall for the little distractions. They're all smoke and mirrors designed to mislead you."

He leaned back in his seat and stared at the floor. "There *is* an enemy that seeks to steal your peace, kill your dreams, and destroy your destiny."

"It sure as heck feels that way," I snorted. "Just as soon as things get tough in business or a relationship . . . anywhere really, I swear other seemingly 'better opportunities' pop up out of nowhere, like freaking weeds. I always have to stop myself from chasing every little random side-hustle. Every time I've gotten side-tracked, I eventually had to learn again that nothing worthwhile comes easy, and I should never have been distracted from my dream in the first place!"

Carl kept looking at the floor but nodded as I spoke.

I continued. "Honestly, I can't even fathom the amount of bad advice I have received over the years—too much to count, and it cost me a lot of time and money. I remember when I was writing my first book . . . I was researching the publishing industry, trying to get some ideas on how to publish my own book because I wasn't going to wait for people to 'discover' me . . ."

Austin's eyebrows shot up when he heard me mention my books, so I stopped to explain my speaking and writing. I learned from a mentor years ago to never downplay my accomplishments, but I wouldn't say I liked the assumptions most people have about me when they know I am an author and speaker.

First, people assume I have "natural creativity" and "ideas" just come to me, so they dismiss the painstaking discipline and effort it takes for a serial procrastinator like me to write and complete a project, all without ever having a guarantee of success. Second, they assume a published book is the finish line, and fame and money begin to flow shortly after, which couldn't be further from the truth. Most people have no idea that for an average author to be successful, a published book is only the beginning of a long journey of writing and marketing, and rarely does an author's first piece of work succeed.

And finally, because I am a motivational speaker, they think I am somehow immune to negativity or insecurity, and they should pretend to be the same way around me. As if I am a drill sergeant who will scream "Be more positive!" the moment they mention a fear or worry. I didn't like to see people pretend everything was okay in front of me because they feared criticism.

I explained to Austin that I simply write and speak about life principles as I learn to incorporate them and that I am far from defeating negativity. But I didn't tell him that fear and negativity were precisely why I was on that train in the first place!

I laughed as I finished telling him about when I first started researching the process. Every article I read about book publishing or marketing mentioned how it is nearly impossible to succeed as a self-published author or speaker if you are not famous. How you might as well expect to sell only a few hundred books and be happy because you probably won't be one of the rare outliers who succeed, and how I hated that sort of limited thinking because it actually deterred me from starting for a very long time.

"Anyways," I continued, "I eventually realized that ordinary people don't take chances because they look at the statistics of success. That's why they are deterred when the odds are stacked against them. That's why they set mediocre goals and live mediocre lives. I learned that extraordinary people do extraordinary things against all odds and despite the statistics. So now, the more I am told something is impossible, or out of reach, the more I want to achieve it."

"That's so good!" Austin adjusted his glasses and listened intently.

"Thank you!" I smiled and continued. "Honestly, asking myself the question, 'What if?' has changed my life. If not for that question, I don't know if I ever would have pursued my dream."

I looked at Carl, "Carl, you'll probably agree with this. It seems that . . . when you set out to achieve something big, you've got to make two decisions. First," I held out my thumb, "You have to be brutally honest with yourself that it may take a very long time, so you've got to resolve to see it all the way through."

Then I extended my pointer finger, "And second, at the same time, you've got to decide to believe like a child that what you are working on could blow up into massive success any day! Because how could you ever persist through all of the ups and downs, if you don't believe it could happen for you . . . even if you have to be a bit naive and unrealistic sometimes?"

"Always!" Carl nearly shouted. "Always. What other way is there to live? If you don't have hope for tomorrow, you will drown in your own despair. That's how we survived those grueling days of the war . . . just a little hope that tomorrow might be a better day, tomorrow might bring an end to the suffering."

***

The train rocked along the tracks. We were somewhere in between Sandpoint, Idaho and Libby, Montana. I guessed we had already crossed the state line. I pulled aside the thick curtain to take a peek outside, it was mostly dark, but the looming silhouettes of the mountains were visible through the blur of snowflakes swirling past the window. There were no city lights, highways, or streetlamps, just forests, mountains, and a tempest of snow.

I leaned back and sunk into the couch, pulling my sweater tight around my neck to get even cozier. *Could there be a better setting than this for a glass of whiskey and a good conversation?* I doubted it.

I admired what Carl had said about having hope that "tomorrow might bring an end to suffering." Most of us in today's world weren't suffering at war. We weren't in England, France, or Germany in the 1940s getting our homes bombed or being herded like sheep into concentration camps, but still, even in this modern and prosperous world, people were suffering in their own way.

There was man-made suffering, and then there was *mind*-made suffering. One was external, brought on by circumstances we couldn't control, and the other was internal, and this suffering we *could* end by choosing to no longer be consumed by fear of failure and worry about the future.

If we could truly understand the power of hope and learn to place it on greater things, millions of people could be free of all the suffering from lack of purpose, complacency, and mediocrity.

I remembered that old biblical proverb, *where there is no vision, the people perish.* What a convicting truth. Because if there is no vision, there can be no hope; without hope, people perish.

How many precious hours of life are wasted because people are tormented by the fear of opinions and criticism and simply conform to society?

When I was sitting in that cubicle at my old job, rotting away with no direction, purpose, or hope for the future, I experienced some of my darkest days. But everything changed instantly when I discovered books and allowed myself to dream again! That's all it took. That's all a person needs. You can take everything from a man but his dream. And if he's got a dream, then he's got hope, and hope is all he needs.

I stared out the window and thought of my grandfather.

In those four years he spent in the camps, getting beaten by Nazi guards, starved, and worked to exhaustion in below-freezing temperatures, watching his fellow prisoners being shot in the back of the head just as soon as they collapsed, unable to work or march for another minute, he must have despaired. And yet, he said that what kept him going one day at a time was a hope that any day now, it would all come to an end, that he would see his family again.

Prisoners who held out hope lived until Dachau was liberated, but many who could no longer imagine a different future became weak and perished before liberation.

Sitting there in the cabin at the end of the train, thinking back on those dismal moments of my life, I was reminded again of the power of a dream—what a timely conversation with these two strangers. Og Mandino said *You will be the same person five years from now, except for the books you read and the people you meet.* It was true. I thought I needed alone time, but this accidental meeting was invigorating.

Maybe it's not so accidental.

Lately, I had been trapped in my head. I was thinking too much about myself and my insecurities and losing the vision behind my goals.

I was causing my own suffering. It all began with a dream

to plant in people that seed of hope that was once planted in me, and somehow I let the process become more urgent than the purpose. But if I stayed true to the goal, continued to hope, and believed that even I could do incredible things despite my shortcomings, how could I fail?

I glanced at Austin. He was staring at his feet, now holding a drink.

"Austin, you can't possibly enjoy having doors slammed in your face daily. You must have some big goal to be willing to put up with that." I guessed.

"Honestly, it's not as bad as it seems. I'm not selling things people don't need; I help people improve their homes. Sometimes, if they are lucky, a cozy little home is all people have in this world, especially the older folks, and I look at it as a way to help them preserve a few years on that home." He glanced up at Carl, who was listening, expressionless.

"It doesn't provide a consistent paycheck, but at least I'm living my life on my schedule and not getting yelled at by some boss."

"Yes!" I pumped my fist enthusiastically. I was starting to like this kid even more. "You said it perfectly. Success means *living life on your own terms,* whatever those terms are that you have set for yourself! There is no one definition for success, as long as you live how you want to live."

I raised my glass in Austin's direction for an "air toast" before continuing. "It blows my mind how so many people don't create their own terms for life—people just do what their parents, boss, or friends suggest. It's like being bound by a contract you never signed."

Austin nodded as I spoke, still looking down at his feet. When I finished, he replied softly. "My little girl has cancer. I want to ensure we don't fall behind on the treatment bills our insurance doesn't cover."

Five

"Sometimes all we need is a little perspective"

The train pulled into the station in Libby and trembled to an abrupt stop. The brakes released with a loud hiss that sent snow swirling into the air from under the wheels.

For the last half-hour, Austin and Carl had continued to talk about Austin's little girl, but I'd stayed silent because I was trying to figure out how to remove the size ten-and-a-half sneakered foot out of my mouth. I put myself into these situations often; you would think I knew when to shut up by now. I had a strong opinion about everything and, because of it, could say inconsiderate things and had to learn many lessons the hard way.

When will I learn to keep my mouth shut and not pretend to know everything, especially when people like Austin live these nightmares?

I was babbling on about living life on my terms while this poor young salesman from Chicago was trying to save his little girl. Of course, as I was ranting, I had in mind people who lived sedentary lives, going whichever way the wind blew and not pursuing anything, but I wished I had known his circumstance before I mouthed off.

I had a thousand things to say to those wasting their time away, yet I couldn't think of a single encouraging word to offer when it mattered most. I just sat and watched as Carl lovingly nodded and listened to the kid.

"Sometimes, all we need is a little perspective," Carl spoke up loudly, looking directly at me. I snapped out of the lecture I was giving myself and tried to swallow the lump in my throat. He must have noticed my silence and wanted to ensure I caught the embedded message. *"How significant do your little problems feel now?"* he seemed to be saying. I could see it in his eyes.

"When you have a problem, it feels like no one or nothing else in the world matters. Right?"

Austin and I bobbed our heads in agreement.

He continued, "How can you care about the needs of others if your problem consumes you? Of course, it's easy to think that if only this problem disappeared, we would be happy. But isn't that a little naive? The next one will be upon us in a matter of time. That's life.

"Every winter brings an end to summer's bloom, but the empty flower garden has a fresh start by next spring. So it is with problems, like changing seasons, they may feel desolate at the moment, but they bring new things into your life that you otherwise would not have room for. The old needs to be tilled and uprooted before something new can grow.

"But . . . if you see life as a series of problems which you must avoid at all costs, if you tip-toe around just praying things don't fall apart, you will be timid. What extraordinary things can you achieve if you haven't built up resilience? None! Fulfillment comes from solving your problems, not avoiding them."

Carl leaned his cane against his knee and folded his arms. "Don't wish for a life without problems; find opportunities for a fresh start in the midst of your problems . . . that's how you grow. And if you think you can't possibly handle something any longer, perhaps a little change in perspective can help you bear the discomfort for just a little bit longer.

"There is always someone who would gladly trade places with you and take on your troubles. If you don't believe me, take a walk in a cemetery, and you'll meet hundreds of people who would eagerly take your place."

"Yes, sir," Austin joined in. "That's the way I try to see it. I still have time with my little girl and am believing for a miracle that she will be healthy again . . . some people no longer have that with their families."

Carl closed his eyes and inhaled deeply. His lower lip quivered. "Mmhmm," he groaned. "Yes, some people no longer have time with their loved ones." He gently touched the thin gold band around his ring finger.

Suddenly I wished I hadn't left Makenzie to spend Christmas without me. In recent months I had undoubtedly lost perspective. There was always something taking my attention, some deadline hanging over my head, some meeting or call or engagement approaching, or a book I was working on and promoting. I was always anticipating future success and happiness; *soon, everything will take off, soon, I won't have to stress about income, and soon I'll have more time for family trips,* I told myself. But I was neglecting the many blessings in my life. I couldn't remember the last time I thanked God for everything I already had.

In one of my old journals, I had paraphrased an assignment that Og Mandino gave his audiences when he delivered a speech.

"Every time you start to feel sorry for yourself, and you feel the need to go into your closet and hide from this big mean world, just pull out a sheet of paper, you big baby, and take a quick inventory of all the blessings you have in your life.

Your eyes—how much money would you take for your eyes? How about your ears—would you sell your ability to hear? How about your hands and feet—would you take a large sum of money for those? What about your sound mind—would you trade that in for a few million bucks?"

Then the old man would delicately pull out a worn-out card from his wallet and read this poem.

The World is Mine

Today upon a bus I saw a girl with golden hair;

She seemed so gay, I envied her, and wished that I were half so fair;

I watched her as she rose to leave, and saw her hobble down the aisle.

She had one leg and wore a crutch, but as she passed—a smile.

Oh, God, forgive me when I whine;

I have two legs—the world is mine.

Later on I bought some sweets. The boy who sold them had such charm,

I thought I'd stop and talk awhile. If I were late, t'would do no harm.

And as we talked he said, "Thank you, sir, you've really been so kind.

It's nice to talk to folks like you because, you see, I'm blind."

Oh, God, forgive me when I whine;

I have two eyes—the world is mine.

Later, walking down the street, I met a boy with eyes so blue.

But he stood and watched the others play; it seemed he knew not what to do.

I paused, and then I said, "Why don't you join the others, dear?"

But he looked straight ahead without a word, and then I knew, he couldn't hear.

Oh, God, forgive me when I whine;

I have two ears—the world is mine.

Two legs to take me where I go,

Two eyes to see the sunset's glow,

Two ears to hear all I should know,

Oh, God, forgive me when I whine;

I'm blessed, indeed, the world is mine.

I needed to go back and read that journal entry again, never to forget it.

It's a funny thing . . . how is it that since childhood, we've been taught about the principle of gratitude, and yet, somehow, we still don't seem to get it? Somehow, our little problems keep us moping, groaning, and complaining through life.

Problems kept me focused on my past, and opportunities kept me focused on my future, but moments like this gave me a little perspective on my present.

"I'm blessed; indeed, the world is mine," I whispered.

The train gently lurched forward as I headed back for the last cabin. There had been a line near the restrooms, and I considered running into the station, but just before I stepped out, there was a final boarding call, and the remaining passengers rushed out of the Libby station back to the train. To my surprise, much of the train seemed to have emptied throughout the stops between Vancouver and Libby. There were few passengers scattered throughout the cars as I passed through.

By the time I made my way back to the cabin at the end of the train, Austin had moved to the opposite couch and sat next to Carl, who was holding a faded black and white photo of a young girl. The old man's enormous smile said it all as he handed it to Austin.

"That's my Betty—she is only seventeen in this photo. She gave it to me before I left for Europe. It used to smell like her perfume, but after riding with me in the tank through the war and all these years later, it probably doesn't smell so good anymore," he chuckled.

"Wow, I can't believe you still have it after all this time, Carl." Austin carefully held the photograph in his palm.

"Yep, before I left, I promised her that if I returned, I would marry her the minute she was in my arms again, and that's exactly what I did. If you find yourself a good girl, don't waste any time! That's what us smart fellas did. All the other boys who wanted to play around and have some fun for a while, well, they got what was left after all the good girls were taken when it was time to settle down, and they always ended up with the floozies. I guess you get what you wish for."

Austin and I laughed hard as Carl slid the photo into a laminated sleeve and stuck it in his worn leather wallet. The kid pulled his phone out and swiped through pictures of his wife and little girl. Carl squinted at one.

"Yes, yes, you have a nice little family there, Austin. Make every moment you have with those girls count. Nothing can replace the time you spend away from them, nothing."

Carl was looking at me again. As if he knew Austin got it but wasn't so sure I did. And I couldn't disagree with him.

"What about you, Michael," he said. "Aren't you going to show off your sweetheart?"

I smiled and pulled out my phone. "That's Makenzie right there, sir." I showed him a few recent photos of

Makenzie and me on a muddy hike in the Columbia River Gorge several weeks earlier.

"She's the best," I said. "Good for my ego."

She really was the best life and business partner I could ask for. In fact, she was probably on her laptop right now, fighting for our dreams as I sat sipping whiskey with my new friends. Sometimes she worked harder on our goals than I did, hammering away at emails, and trying to book my speaking schedule.

"She believes I'm the greatest writer and speaker in the world, and people just don't know it yet—so she's taken it upon herself to prove it."

"You are fortunate to have a lady like that. It's difficult for anyone to be great without the support of their spouse," said Carl.

"Ha! Absolutely," I scoffed. "I know a lot of guys who work from morning to night while their wife is blowing their hard-earned money on fancy brunches and birthday parties for their one-year-olds that cost more than my entire wedding!"

Austin pushed his glasses up on his nose, "Imagine trying so hard to keep up with your friends that it costs you time with your family. People are crazy today . . . life can be falling apart behind closed doors, but *'As long as I have the cute photos to post on social media. . .'*" He tried his best to mimic a ditzy woman's voice.

"It was no different in my day," Carl snorted. "We didn't have all the social stuff you kids have, but people were the same. A guy and his wife could be at each other's throats all week, throwing dishes and ready to kill each other, but still show up to church on Sunday looking like angels for the sake of carrying an appearance.

"You can't judge people—we all have our downfalls—but you can certainly learn a lot by observing."

He nodded in my direction, "Have you any children?"

I shook my head 'no' and took a sip of my Old Fashioned. I didn't mind people asking me when or if I was planning on having any kids, but I didn't like trying to explain myself because not many understood my reasoning. When Makenzie and I got married, we agreed that we'd wait a few years . . . and now that a few years had passed, we were talking about it a lot.

"To be honest, I'm scared as hell, Carl. Not afraid to *have* children . . . I can't imagine living this life without that experience. Children are a blessing—I can see that just by observing friends and family who have had kids . . . and I loved growing up in a big family.

"I'm afraid if we have kids now, I won't become who I want to be. At least it would be much harder to." I held up my palm as if Carl or Austin would object because usually, at this point, people jumped in to tell me how wrong I was.

The truth was I saw many of my peers encouraging their kids to do and become whatever they want, yet the parents have taken no risks in their lives and live in their comfort zone. It's like people wish the world for their children but then use those same kids as an excuse for why they haven't pursued their own dreams! If you tell your kid that they can be and do everything they dream up, but your kid sees you comfortable on your ass in front of the TV every night eating Cheetos, year after year, they will become *you,* not who you wish them to be.

I knew that wouldn't work for me.

I slowly rotated my half-empty glass in my hand, expecting Carl or maybe Austin to respond. But they both were silent. So I continued.

"When he was my age, my dad left the Soviet Union with my mom and seven children in his care and no place to go. All he knew was that America had freedom and opportunities for us kids to do something with our lives. He bet on himself. I mean, can you take a bigger risk than that?"

The two men were still listening. "So when we were young, Dad never had to tell us that we could do anything we put our minds to—we knew we could because we saw how my parents fought for their dreams. But that's rare. You don't see that in the average person."

All around me, I saw people who were far too

comfortable and blind to the opportunity around them. They were taking no risks, doing nothing extraordinary, and complaining about their circumstances, the government, or the economy. These same people claim they'll teach their kids to do great things. Like hell they will.

I looked at these two men who'd presumably never felt this way and tried to explain:

"I feel like I am stuck in 'no man's land.' Like I'm already halfway to where I want to be, past the point of no return, and having children could completely disrupt my momentum. When I do something, I go all in . . . I've always been that way. It would be tough to divide my energy between kids and my dream. But at the same time, it's not right for me to keep Makenzie from the joy I know she would experience in being a mother."

I thought of Makenzie and how connected she was with her nieces and nephews and how she practically melted around babies. Knowing I was keeping her from having her own every time I saw her with a kid just added pressure. Honestly, I wished I could take it off the table for a few more years. Just to reach my goals, and then once I established myself as an author and speaker, then we'd have children.

"But as you both know, pausing time is not a power any of us have!" I felt my voice break and stopped talking.

I succeeded in keeping myself from crying, but I know the two of them noticed the tears in my eyes. *Time,* I just wished I had more time. I wished I had started earlier. I wished I didn't waste my early twenty's living carelessly. I wished I could take those days back.

I wouldn't quit. I couldn't quit now. I wanted more time to properly experience every part of this gift we call 'life.' I felt it was getting away from me, like I had to choose between my dreams and settling down. I admit I had a pretty black-and-white perspective on the idea. Still, I could only picture two future scenarios for my life at that moment: I would either be Michael, the author, and speaker who accomplished his dreams, or Michael, the dad with a beer belly and lawnmower who quit on his big dreams. The latter depressed me.

I took a breath to reel in my emotions and continued. "Call me selfish. Call me whatever you want, but I would never forgive myself if I quit and then spent the rest of my life justifying my decision and making excuses for why I settled and abandoned my dream, or worse . . . blame and grow resentful towards my wife and kids."

I remembered the time when I was still stuck in my cubicle years ago, miserable and hopeless, and the promise I made to God. I debated sharing that private covenant I made, but everything was out in the open now, so I continued.

"Years ago, I prayed every day for God just to nudge me

in the right direction. I swore if He gave me an opportunity, I would go after it with everything I had and never waste another day of my life again. He held up his part of the bargain, and I have to hold up mine. I just don't want it to come at the sacrifice of losing out on everything else."

Carl smiled, "If that's how you feel, you forgot who you made a bargain with!"

Before Carl could elaborate, the cabin door opened, and the conductor stepped in. The heavyset older man wore a snug navy blue vest, matching pressed slacks, and a tall round cap with a shiny black bill. With his gold-rimmed glasses and white beard, he looked like Santa at his day job.

Six

"Don't wait to be discovered"

Oren was the name engraved on the metal tag pinned to his chest. For a moment, he looked annoyed, but when his eyes spotted Carl in his veteran's hat, his demeanor changed instantly.

"Well, you gentlemen look cozy!" he exclaimed. "Technically, you aren't supposed to be here, but if you all promise not to spill your drinks or track in the snow between stops, I never saw you."

"I'll keep an eye on these kids," Carl grinned. "They have been behaving so far."

"Well, good!" Oren replied, "In that case, I'm going to show you guys something you might appreciate." He walked over to the window and pulled a square piece of the panel off the wall beneath it. He leaned on one knee, reached inside the wall, and turned a knob.

"There," he said. "That'll make it nice and toasty. This old baby had had a little upgrade sometime between now and when it was first used a very long time ago. It's got a heating system that's been modified to connect to the modern cars."

"How come this car is attached to this passenger train?" I asked, "Is it being transported somewhere?"

"It is being transported," Oren replied. "Someone is paying a lot of money to have it pulled over to Chicago. That's why it is not supposed to be available for passengers. Once it is ready for service, this car will be an upgraded, costly option for people who like to travel back in time and ride with class. And, of course, the bar will be stocked on those trips." He winked at me.

"Amen to that," I said and lifted my glass.

Oren flung his hands and theatrically spun around until he faced us again. "It makes for a hell of a ride through the Rockies, doesn't it?"

"Yes!" The three of us hollered our agreement in one voice.

"Are you all traveling together?" he asked.

"No, sir," Austin replied. "I guess you could say we were all sort of drawn back here."

"Well, Ok then," Oren said. "I'll check back here in a bit. If you all need refills, just let me know."

"Thank you, Oren. I might take you up on that." I gave him a thumbs-up.

Oren put his hand on Carl's shoulder and smiled, "Thank you for your service, sir!" And with that, he walked out of the cabin.

Not wanting our interrupted conversation to end, I turned to Carl and asked what he meant when he said I forgot who I bargained with. He had me curious.

Carl leaned back and balanced his whiskey on his knee while he pulled his hat back and scratched his bald head. "You two know the story of King Solomon, right?" I nodded and glanced at Austin. Austin nodded as well.

"Good," Carl said. "What did King Solomon ask for?"

"Wisdom," I answered.

I always loved the story of Solomon. When he asked for wisdom and not riches, God granted his request—but also blessed him with riches beyond measure on top of that. Because the great king had been humble and asked for wisdom, he received wisdom and unimaginable wealth.

"Exactly. He asked for wisdom."

Carl pointed his finger at me and then at Austin, who was still sitting next to him. "You see, my ambitious friends, when you do things your own way, you *might* achieve some success and gain some riches. But when you humble yourselves and strive to live with purpose while relying on a greater power for guidance, you will receive everything you set out to achieve and then some. Every day people get the same opportunity King Solomon did. Only most are so obsessed with themselves and don't ask for wisdom. Instead, they ask for riches. That's why they get neither."

Carl looked me square in the eye, and his face became serious. "You, young man, need not worry about choosing between your dreams and your blessings. If you believe you are following your calling, then He will see to it that you don't miss out on any blessings. Leave it be. Let it go. Do what you need to do. And don't even entertain the idea of a plan B. A few kids won't slow a man on a mission; in fact . . . they just might give him that extra motivation he needs!"

I inhaled deeply and smiled, trying to breathe away the rising emotions. With his few simple words, the old man seemed to lighten the weight on my shoulders. I had been too afraid to let go, constantly weighing all of the potential risks and costs of chasing my dream. Perhaps I could finally let it go, let things take their course, and not feel the need to juggle everything simultaneously.

Then Carl turned to Austin, "And you . . . no matter what happens, know that you are doing all you can do and leave the rest up to a power greater than you. You aren't a failure. You've done nothing wrong to deserve this . . . this thing you are living through is out of your control. If you choose to believe in a miracle, then keep believing, damn it! Your thoughts and words have power, especially as a father. A special authority has been given to you. Your family will benefit if you believe and persist. Don't allow the negative to enter your mind."

Carl grabbed Austin's shoulder tightly and shook him gently, "Keep believing, young man. No Plan B"

I purposely avoided looking at the kid. I knew I would lose it if I did. I saw his shoulders shaking from the corner of my eye. I just stared at my feet and prayed for a miracle on Austin's behalf, too.

***

Sometime later, Austin and I were on the back balcony, leaning against the railing. Carl had declined our invitation to get some fresh air. "It's too damn cold out there for me," he laughed, "You boys go ahead and enjoy yourselves."

The snow whipped violently in all directions behind the train. Luckily the overhang above and the side panels on either side protected us from the wind and pelting snow. I didn't know if I had ever been in such frigid temperatures or how long I could last, but the cold was refreshing for the moment. We rumbled over wooden trestle bridges and roaring rivers far below. The sound of the train and wind drowned out any river noise, but we could see the ghostly white rapids churning fiercely.

Besides some light from the train reflecting onto the snow, the terrain was almost entirely dark. Once in a while, we'd spot light from a farmhouse in the distance and then nothing but snow fields and silhouettes of mountains again. Sometimes the mountains were right upon us, and sometimes they loomed in the distance beyond miles and miles of meadows, but they were always there, eerie witnesses to our passage.

After some time, Austin turned to me. "I know that many pro athletes and successful entrepreneurs get into speaking, but how did you do it? Seems like a tough business to break into."

"It was, and it is," I said. "Probably the hardest thing I've ever done. My wife and I started from the bottom, knowing nothing about the industry. Wasn't long before I realized how difficult it is to get hired, especially when nobody knows who you are. I knew it'd be hard, but I also knew I wasn't going to be randomly *discovered,* and I sure as heck wasn't going to wait for that."

"Ha! I know what you mean," Austin laughed. "People always think that anyone who made it just *got lucky* or became an *overnight success* or whatever they call it."

"Yep, you always hear about how some country singer

was *discovered* in a dive bar in Nashville or some actor was *discovered* while waiting tables." I threw air quotes up with my fingers.

"But no one ever hears about how the singers, the actors, the businessmen, the salesmen . . . " I smacked his shoulder, "who worked their asses off year after year and put themselves in a position to be discovered eventually."

I hated the term *overnight success*. It's a term ordinary people use to describe someone who finally achieves their dreams. There is no such thing. They just don't know about the years a person has spent in the dark, working and perfecting their craft when no one was watching, cheering, or paying. If more people realized how much they controlled their own "luck," there would be many more people in this world acting on their dreams and not waiting to be *discovered* or looking for ways to become an *overnight success*.

"In any case," I continued. "I wasn't famous, and I sure as hell didn't know of any back doors into the speaking world . . ."

I told the kid how I got better by practicing short fifteen-minute speeches. I would rent a small conference room back home and invite friends, family, and anybody in the community I could entice to come for the free coffee and donuts. Then I would give my mini speeches. I would always have someone video record me—and learned how to edit the footage so that I could turn those videos into highlight reels. Soon, I had some decent videos and strategically taken pictures of me speaking to an audience. Then I learned how to build a website and added all the videos and photos to look like I was a legitimate speaker.

"Wow," Austin shook his head, "I love that attitude, *'Don't wait to be discovered.'* I'm going to use that."

"Yep. That's a principle I have lived by these last few years. It reminds me to stay on top of things and never make excuses. No matter what I have already accomplished, if I'm not where I want to be yet, I can't sit and wait around for something to happen," I said.

"So then people started taking you seriously and inviting you . . . after you had your website up and you wrote a book?" Austin was curious.

I laughed, "Sheesh, man, I wish! Absolutely *nothing* happened. No one hired me to speak. I had no clue how to market myself. Sure, I had a few friends invite me to speak at small events, and I spoke at those as a favor. But I hadn't booked a paid engagement, so I wasn't technically a professional speaker. I still had a lot of work to do.

"I invested a lot of time and money into programs to learn about the speaking business . . . and of course, you know, Austin, that when an entrepreneur uses the term, 'invested,' it usually means 'wasted' a lot of time and money."

Austin laughed. "Boy, have I 'invested' a lot of money over the years before I settled on selling roofs. I think I have about a thousand boxes of health products in my garage that I stocked up on and never sold."

I slapped his shoulder with the back of my palm, "Yep, yep, so you know what I'm talking about."

"You still get nervous when you speak?" he asked.

"Every time!" I groaned. "Sometimes, just before I am introduced onto the stage, I debate running for the parking lot and getting the hell out of there. The nights before are rough. But I would much rather lose sleep feeling anxious about what is to come the next day than to lose sleep feeling anxious about what isn't.

"At my old job, I had a lot of sleepless nights. Only back then, it was because I dreaded my life. I knew that tomorrow could bring nothing new because I hadn't changed anything today. I knew that tomorrow would be just as miserable as today was because when that alarm clock screamed, I would again fall out of bed, fight traffic to get to the office, and settle in my cubicle for another day of misery."

I crossed my arms and hugged my body to keep warm, but it didn't help much.

"These days, I lose sleep but only because I want to do my best because I don't want to fail or disappoint someone who took a chance on me . . . honestly, I just want to be one of the greatest ever to do it, so I've got to put everything I have into my speeches. In all honesty, that's part of the reason why I took this trip. I've been struggling a lot. I guess you could say after years of chasing this dream, I've become a little scattered, and it has taken a lot out of me . . ." I shrugged, "Sometimes I wish it were a little easier."

"But I will say this though, this conversation with Carl and you . . . it's given me a lot of perspectives."

Austin stared out at the tracks disappearing into the dark behind the train and sighed. "Yeah, there's definitely something special about Carl."

Seven

"You've got to believe it in!"

Oren returned with three drinks on a tray and informed us we would be arriving in Whitefish within the hour. From there, the train would head to West Glacier and on through eastern Montana, but there were reports of delays due to bad weather. When he mentioned the train might make an extended stop in Whitefish, it didn't bother me like it might have other passengers. I wasn't in a hurry to get anywhere.

I noticed something that made me mentally count how many drinks I'd had. When Oren had pushed open the swinging door, I saw that the shelves in the bar cabin were now stacked from top to bottom with liquor. *When did he have time to stock the shelves?* I thought. *Maybe when the kid and I were on the balcony?* I figured we had been so preoccupied in our conversations that we didn't hear the jolly conductor furnishing the bar, although how odd that we hadn't noticed him doing it. I guessed he figured it would be easier to keep us supplied straight from the cabin next door instead of running drinks through the train. But he was a conductor, not a waiter . . . I wondered why he had gone to the trouble for us.

Carl and I chatted about touch screen phones, politics, and a distillery I visited while on a speaking trip in Kentucky. I told him how a few of us, who had gone on the trip together, separated from the tour group and explored the entire warehouse on our own. The ten-story building must have been at least a hundred years old, and apart from the old plank walkways around the perimeter of each floor, the whiskey barrels stacked on top of each other filled the entire building from the first floor all the way up to the top floor. The barrels were so coated in dust and cobwebs that it was nearly impossible to see the logos burned into them.

Carl excitedly explained the aging process I had seen on my trip. He told me the barrels would be roasted and charred to draw out the wood's natural sugars before the whiskey was even poured into them. How the whiskey aged in the barrels for years and how the Kentucky climate helped with the aging process. He talked about how the used barrels were then sold to wineries, breweries, and other liquor distilleries to be reused for their own operation and wouldn't be accepted by certain brands unless the barrels went through that exact sequence of use. Certain flavors of wine, beer, or liquor couldn't be replicated exactly unless the barrels were previously used to age whiskey.

How foolish of me. I had assumed we were talking strictly about whiskey until the old man winked at me. "There's a recipe for success just like there is a recipe for disaster . . . you just got to make sure you have the right ingredients. Once you do, all you can do is trust the process, even if it takes longer than you want. Like aging whiskey, good things take time."

It made me appreciate the drink I held even more.

Austin was standing in the far corner of the cabin. *Probably still trying to get warm next to that heater,* I thought. He had pulled the drapes apart but wasn't looking at anything in particular as he stared into the darkness. His forehead was scrunched; I could tell he was deep in thought.

These two strangers were beginning to feel like old friends. Typically if I was stuck in a conversation that stayed surface-level and the topic never deepened beyond TV shows, the weather, or current events, I'd try to find a way out of it. Whether it was on an airplane, in a coffee shop, or on a train, I hated small talk. However, tonight's conversations were stimulating. I voiced frustrations and fears, was challenged, had to think from a different perspective on a few occasions, and even felt stupid a time or two. These types of conversations were priceless.

This is how Iron sharpens Iron, I concluded.

In today's world, where everyone competes to be the greatest victim, we could use tougher conversations. People preferred to be coddled rather than challenged. Some change in ideas could do us good.

It was as if the three of us were gathered at the right place, at the right time in our lives, and when we needed it most . . . at least when I needed it most.

After some time, Austin sat on the couch next to me, fiddling with his fingers. I could tell he had something on his mind; he kept glancing in my direction impatiently while Carl and I spoke. When there was a break in our conversation, the kid pushed his thick glasses up on his nose and jumped on the opportunity.

"Michael, I hope you don't mind if I change the subject back to what we talked about earlier . . ." He hesitated. "What do you say to yourself when you are ready to get up and speak if you're not *feeling* confident? In our sales training meetings, we get pretty hyped, yelling affirmations and pumping each other up, but honestly, by the time I'm in front of a customer a few hours later, all the hype is gone, and I'm back to feeling nervous."

I laughed. "Oh man, I'm not a fan of hype."

I had learned from attending a lifetime of church services and dozens of events with motivational speakers that anyone can feel good for a few minutes, but those feel-good emotions disappear pretty quickly when it comes time to take action. In fact, every time I spoke to an audience, I started by asking for a commitment; I would teach and inspire to the best of my ability, and they would take immediate action on what they learned. That was the deal.

"So you're telling me you don't dance around the room with your wife and chest bump each other before you sit down to write?" A big smile crossed the kid's face as he waited for my answer.

I chuckled, "No, but sometimes I beat my chest and holler like a gorilla!"

I looked at the old man, "Carl, I'm sure you heard of Jim Rohn?"

"Of course!" Carl smiled, "I saw him speak in Dallas once when a company I worked for took us to one of his seminars."

"This reminds me of what he says about affirmations and motivation," I continued.

I told them how I tried to model my speeches after the greats like Jim Rohn. He used to say that *"affirmation without application is the beginning of delusion."* Affirmations are powerful; you can reprogram your subconscious mind and change your life by changing your self-talk. But it must absolutely be followed by action. Nothing changes if you sit and affirm extraordinary things, but your actions reflect your old, mediocre self, not what you have declared.

It's the same with motivation. You can get hyped and feel good for a time, but you can't sustain yourself on hype. The motivation has got to come from much deeper within, not just from a momentary exciting feeling. Inspiration is abundant out there these days, and yet few people actually change. People rely on the excitement, but just as quickly as you can get your head in the clouds, you can get brought down to your knees if you only rely on *feeling* motivated.

Austin listened attentively and nodded as I explained.

"One of the funniest things I've ever heard from Jim's seminar tape recordings was when he talked about motivation. He'd often say, 'If you take a guy who is an idiot, and you motivate him, you don't create a successful person; you just have yourself a motivated idiot.'"

Austin and Carl laughed. "Spot on," Carl added.

"Yep, that's why I'm not a fan of hype," I continued. "I don't like motivational speakers who scream and shout until your ear drums are hurting, but by the end of the day, all you remember is that you felt good, but you forget what you were feeling good about. There's very little practical advice. Jim Rohn, Og Mandino, Zig Ziglar . . . all those great speakers gave people applicable real-life principles and then used inspirational stories to drive the message home. That has a lasting impact, long after the sixty-minute speech is over and everyone has gone home."

As I talked, I could feel the butterflies in my stomach just thinking about the next time I'd be taking the stage.

"So, I still don't get how you get yourself over the nervousness," said Austin.

"Before every speaking engagement, I tell myself that *I'm ready*. I say those words out loud, and I write them on my wrist, on my whiteboard in my office, and on sticky notes where I can see them daily. I know that I have done everything I can to prepare for that moment, and the only thing left for me to do is to step on stage and give the people my all."

"Sure . . ." I continued. "Later, I will be a better writer, later, I will be a better speaker with more experience, but right now, I'm ready because I've done everything I possibly can to get here. Otherwise, fear sets in, and that's why, Austin, you probably get nervous when you are in front of a customer. When you give yourself too much time to mull over your skills and abilities, you forget about all the things you've done to prepare yourself, and you're only thinking of their potential objections . . . now you're back to feeling inferior. Of course, you'll be nervous.

"Now, don't get me wrong. By no means have I mastered this yet. In fact, part of the reason I'm on this trip in the first place has to do with my own fears . . . but I wouldn't be where I'm at today if I hadn't done this for myself."

I grabbed him by the shoulder. "The next time you're standing in front of a prospect's door, remind yourself of how far you've come. Remember a successful sale from the past, the face of a previous grateful customer, the hours you have put in to study your product or service, and say, 'I'm ready for this moment just as I am. I'm ready.'"

As I was speaking to Austin, my own words echoed in my head. I was advising this kid about confidence and overcoming fears because of how much I had grown over the years. I was speaking from experience, not theory. I was more equipped than I had recently been giving myself credit for.

How did I forget about my victories? *By being careless,* I concluded. *By failing to be intentional with my own principles.*

One of the most powerful habits I developed over the years has been to wake in the morning and journal everything I am grateful for. I used to list my successes, blessings, skills, and strengths. This routine alone had given me tremendous confidence in myself. But now I couldn't remember the last morning I had done that.

No wonder I hadn't been able to shake myself free of the slump I was in. Somewhere along the way, I got caught up in the grind and had forgotten to lean on my own experience, remember my own successes, and acknowledge how far I had come. Here I was, spending Christmas Eve on a train far from everyone I loved because my own life vision had become murky, and my confidence in my dream had diminished.

I was telling this kid precisely what he needed to do to master his fears, yet I had forgotten about what got me here in the first place.

Sometimes it is easier to give an encouraging word to another than it is to accept it for ourselves, I thought.

Austin leaned with his elbows on his knees and his knuckles under his chin and stared at the green carpet.

"And what if I'm not ready? I mean, right now, there is a huge opportunity in my company. If I took it, I would be presenting to large contractors at trade shows and even speaking at conferences. That's why I wanted to ask about how you get the confidence to speak . . . I'd have to get comfortable with speaking, which scares the hell out of me, but the pay is incredible, and I wouldn't be selling door to door. I'm just afraid to ask about it . . . I don't want to make a fool of myself."

"You've got to believe it IN!" Carl hollered, squeezing his weathered hand in a tight fist and punching the air. "It's one thing to believe something good will happen to you *someday*. It's a different thing entirely to believe it *into* existence."

Austin quickly straightened his posture. "Yes, sir," he said.

I barely kept myself from laughing. It was like watching a drill sergeant scare a new recruit.

"Before you got here, Austin," Carl continued, "Michael was telling me about his fears with speaking, and he's been speaking for some time. The fear of failure doesn't go away. It will always be in the back of your mind—just remember that courage would not exist without fear! If you wait until you are no longer afraid, or until you feel ready, that opportunity will be long gone."

"That's exactly right," I added. "I know it's what I need to do, so I just do it scared. If that position in your company is what you want, go get it!"

Both Carl and I were taking turns encouraging the kid. *I guess that's what you get when you have a likable personality; people want you to succeed.* Austin had that. I would have liked to see the kid succeed even had I not known about his little girl. Some people won't give you a chance to finish your sentence before they fire off an excuse. It was refreshing to see someone so open-minded to possibility.

Clearly the whiskey had done its job on the old man. He was loose and gesturing with his hands, I was expecting him to spill his drink any second, but he somehow managed not to splash a single drop on the spotless antique carpet.

"Start acting like it is impossible to fail!" Carl's voice boomed. He instantly reminded me of another old speaker I admired, Norman Vincent Peale.

"Start living as if you are already in that position and doing it well. See yourself on stage. See yourself closing the deals. Hear the applause. Feel the pats on the back. That's how you believe it in. The mind attracts to itself whatever it believes to be true! And belief does not come after the feeling of fear has gone—it exists despite the fears."

The old man set his glass on the floor between his feet and tossed his cane on the couch next to him.

"Imagine this," he said, pointing to his temples. "You can change the brain. The biggest disabilities you have are your beliefs. It's not your skills, or your finances, or your luck. When some misfortune happens, you ponder on that experience over and over. You feel the pain a thousand times, as if you are still living it . . . even when you're home safe behind closed doors, the failure stays with you. You imagine the past and feel it now. In a matter of time, those feelings of despair form into a belief even if it may not be true, and suddenly you behave like that fearful failure of a person."

He tapped his head as he spoke, "I'm broke, I'm dumb, I don't belong, I'm awkward, I'm shy, I'm not qualified, on and on . . . wiring the brain for failure!"

Carl shifted forward until he sat just on the cushion's edge. "So . . . if you can change your brain to believe that you are a failure because of one misfortune, don't you think you can change your thinking and start to believe you are *already* a success by imagining future success!? By feeling the emotion and seeing the success, even before you've done it?"

Before Austin or I could respond, Carl shouted, "Of course, you can! The brain is an instrument . . . a machine. It doesn't know the difference between something you imagine or experience. It believes the experience is happening now and responds accordingly. Worry deteriorates your mind, and enthusiasm gives it life! Enthusiasm for the future, that's what it means to believe it in!"

I thought back to earlier that morning, how my mind never stopped racing. I thought back to the hours spent in worry and distress.

It's time to pay a bit more attention to what I continually believe into my life!

Carl dropped his hands to his knees and looked at the ground for a moment before he spoke in a low voice. "So many say, 'Old dogs can't learn new tricks.' But on a television program I watched, they're talking about something called 'neuroplasticity.' And guess what?" He lifted his head and looked at Austin, "Turns out old dogs *can* learn new tricks. The mind does not stop growing if you don't stop feeding it. The mind does not stop bringing to you everything you hold in it, be it positive or negative."

Then he smiled big, "Even at my age, there are many things I'm still trying to believe into existence."

"I've got some bad news, boys," Oren announced as he stepped into the cabin. "We're staying put here in Whitefish for the next few hours and possibly overnight until the tracks are cleared. An avalanche covered the tracks in the mountain pass somewhere between West Glacier and Essex."

Eight

"Faith without action is dead; action activates miracles"

"Well, *now* it's time to get some fresh air," Carl murmured and got up slowly.

"I'll join you!" I jumped up to help the old man up. We stopped by my room to grab the coat Makenzie had suggested I bring along for the trip. I told her I wouldn't need it since I would be staying on the train, but she had insisted, and now I was glad she did.

I had flipped through the Amtrak magazine earlier and read up on the town.

Whitefish was one of those classic timber and mining towns that hadn't grown much over the last century, one of the thousands scattered all over the country you stumble upon every now and then when taking a road trip. These days, the fascinating little town attracts skiers, hikers, and beer drinkers who flood in every year to play in the national parks, "shred the mountain" at the ski resort and patronize the breweries.

On this evening, it looked extra magical with big Edison bulbs and red bells strung on wires across the street, zig-zagging from building to building for several blocks. Central Avenue looked like the inside of Santa's workshop, with wreaths and candy canes on the lampposts, snowmen, and angels painted on the glass of every store window, and dozens of bundled-up people milling around. Most of the businesses in the tiny downtown were still occupying the original red brick and plank board buildings from the old days, all right up against each other. I wondered if someone climbing on the roof of a building on one end of Central Avenue could get to the other end of the block by jumping from roof to roof.

With nearly a foot of snow on the ground and more steadily falling from the sky, I carefully navigated our route down the sidewalk from the station, trying to keep my sneakers from slipping while simultaneously helping Carl stay upright. Within a block, even my socks were soaked.

Carl balanced himself with his cane in one hand, and his other arm wrapped tightly around my elbow. "Shit, this might have been easier if we hadn't drunk all that whiskey!"

I laughed hard. "Speak for yourself, Carl, I'm feeling just fine, but *you're* definitely having a rough time out here. I guess some people just can't handle whiskey!" I teased.

"Yeah, yeah," he muttered sarcastically, "A few decades ago, you wouldn't have been able to keep up with me at the bar."

We took cover under an overhang in front of a coffee shop. Christmas music blared over the outdoor speakers of the crowded establishment. The aroma of coffee overpowered the smell of cigars from Carl's jacket. I looked over at the old man, "Did you have anywhere in particular you wanted to go, Carl? Do you want to go inside the shop and get warm? Grab a coffee?"

Carl looked in the shop and then down the street. He hesitated and then asked me for the time. "It's 7:15," I replied, looking at my phone.

He was silent for a few moments and then pointed at my phone. "Does that thing have one of those magical maps where you can look things up here in town?"

"Yes, sir," I smiled. "What would you like me to look up with my magical powers?"

"A church," Carl replied. "There's got to be an evening Christmas service somewhere in this town."

I was surprised by the request and scrolled through my phone. I quickly found a church just off of lively Central

Avenue, a few blocks away. We began our slow-going journey. When we got to within sight of the church, just far enough away from the cheerful greeters welcoming people in, I stopped. I didn't want to have to explain that I was only helping the old man to the church and would not be attending.

"I'll find somewhere I can hang out for a bit and meet you back here after service so I can help you back to the train." I patted Carl's shoulder, but the old man did not let go of my elbow.

"You're not coming in?" he asked. "Oren said the chances of the train leaving anytime tonight were slim, so we have time. He said something about you getting an update on your phone when it is ready."

"No, that's okay," I replied. "I would rather hang out somewhere else, honestly. You go ahead. I'll be right here when you come out."

Carl still did not let go of my elbow. He looked me in the eyes, and I forced a smile. Why was I feeling so guilty? I didn't owe him an explanation. I looked at the flakes collecting on the bill of his hat. "You better hurry, Carl, before you turn into a snowman."

I tried to divert his stare away from me by pointing toward the old brick theater building that had been converted into a church.

After a minute, Carl gently released his grip on my elbow.

"Suit yourself, young man," he said dryly as he headed towards the greeters.

I was not interested in being in a church this evening, or any evening in the near future for that matter. Although I believed in the power of community, and I certainly believed in God, lately, I had been repulsed by the idea of sitting in a room full of people who I felt didn't understand me. But it was more than that . . .

Every Sunday, people gathered to hear a message about God's extraordinary plans for their lives and to expect miracles. They cheered and nodded when they were told there were no limits to what they could do if they pursued their calling. But then, on Monday, most people returned to their routine and never thought twice about putting their God-given dreams, talents, and abilities into action. I knew it wasn't a fair judgment; not all people who attended church were indifferent. And they were certainly no worse off than anyone who didn't participate in a church, for that matter; mediocre people could be found in a church or a dive bar.

But at that time, my frustrations with my own dreams repelled me from spending intimate time with anyone who wasn't eager for success like I was. I hated to see people who believed in a miracle worker and lived with an endless list of excuses.

I couldn't afford to be around folks who acted foolishly with their time and finances all week and then expected miracles on Sunday, treating God like a genie. That was a poor man's mindset, I believed. What was the difference between that and buying a lottery ticket every week, hoping to somehow miraculously fix all the credit card debt you've accrued over the years? There wasn't a difference as far as I could tell. These were the people that were supposed to be an example to the world—of wisdom, courage, discipline, growth . . . not conformity, victimhood, and lethargy.

I saw how people used their faith in God as an excuse to stay comfortable. Because the minute things got uncomfortable or challenging, they would say something like, "Sometimes God just closes doors," or "I feel like this is where God wants me right now." The sayings were actually cop-outs because they were so often used conveniently in defense of "safe" decisions when, really, a hard decision needed to be made.

And what if God needs you somewhere else, but you're too damn scared to get off your butt?

It was a big reason for why I grew up feeling guilty for wanting to be financially successful . . . as if it was somehow wrong for me to not want to live paycheck to paycheck. And I was done with that.

Some people thought the government would fix their problems; some thought God would do it. I was just aware that time was ticking, and I needed to accomplish what I was inspired to do, and neither God nor the government nor my friends or church would do it for me. It was up to me. I've never met anyone who experienced a breakthrough or a miracle sitting on the couch. *Faith without action is dead; action activates miracles.* Church-going people should understand that better than anyone on the planet.

Success requires a deep look within and reflection on my own habits and choices—all those were things *I* was in control of. God plants the seeds, but we must water them or let them dry out. I couldn't judge anyone else—I had plenty of my own destructive tendencies. I just didn't want to be in an environment that encouraged people to leave their problems at God's feet, Sunday after Sunday, and did not teach them how to take responsibility for the decisions that led to those problems in the first place. People didn't seem to understand their actions were preaching louder than their words.

Plus, I was tired of the soft messages.

As I headed back towards the center of town, I glanced over my shoulder to see if Carl had made it to the door. The greeters hadn't noticed the old man struggling down the obstructed sidewalk in the falling snow. He had only made it a few steps from where I had left him and was now standing alone, clearly afraid to take another step.

Crap. I headed back, swearing to myself the entire way

that I would walk him into the church, get him settled, and then leave.

The warm, cozy building allowed my frozen toes to thaw for a few minutes. We then helped ourselves to coffee at the stand before making our way through the double doors, collecting the evening program from a smiling curly-haired lady with a gentle voice. I took my time leading Carl down the sloped aisle way between the rows of empty theater seats. We were early, so I decided I would at least stay long enough to finish my coffee so the old man wouldn't be sitting alone when service started.

About a quarter of the way down the center aisle, I stopped, pointing at a row of seats to our left. "Will this do, Carl?" I asked, hoping he didn't want to be closer to the stage.

"That'll be fine," he replied. We pushed the old folded seats down and sat right next to the aisle. I sat on the edge in case I decided I needed a "bathroom break" and escape. A temporary stage had been constructed below the worn crimson curtains, and when the seats finally filled, a nervous group of teenagers dressed in matching blue choir gowns assembled on the platform. I looked around the theater and up to the balcony above us—not an empty seat in the building.

When the choir had arranged itself into position, a man

climbed up the side steps of the platform and approached the microphone. His face was covered in severe burn scars. The chatter of the packed room quieted as the audience turned their attention to the man on the stage. He didn't speak. He stood quietly and focused his eyes somewhere on the theater's back wall.

A few moments passed, and the lights dimmed, but the man stood silent in the spotlight beam. People around me squirmed in their seats. I would probably be doing the same if I hadn't had those drinks on the train, but instead, I patiently waited, curious to see how this would play out. As a speaker myself, I knew what to watch for and noticed his hands hanging at his sides, shaking. The man was very nervous.

Oh boy. This dude is about two seconds away from running off the stage.

And then he began to sing.

"O Holy Night!

The stars are brightly shining

It is the night of our dear Savior's birth!

Long lay the world in sin and error pining

Till he appeared and the soul felt its worth.

A thrill of hope, the weary soul rejoices

For yonder breaks a new and glorious morn!

Fall on your knees

Oh hear the angel voices

Oh night divine

Oh night, when Christ was born

Oh night divine

Oh night divine

There wasn't a crack or shake in his voice. No hesitation. Nothing held back. This timid mouse suddenly transformed into a roaring lion. His words permeated the room, vibrated off the back wall, and sank into every heart in the room, including mine. I felt the goosebumps on my arms and gripped my coffee with both hands to keep them from trembling.

In a moment's time, I relived every Christmas of my thirty-three years on earth.

I remembered the story my dad told us around the dinner table of his first Christmas in the United States. How my grandpa, even though he was a World War II veteran, had been constantly harassed by the KGB for leading church services in the Soviet Union, and how my uncles were thrown in prison as a way to intimidate him. Dad walked into a grocery store in Vancouver and heard Christian Christmas music playing over the speaker system . . . in the store! In a public place! He couldn't believe that he was in a country that allowed its citizens to practice their faith.

I remembered Christmas when I was six years old, and our family got a call from a local church asking for the names and ages of all the children in the household. Someone had tipped them off that a large immigrant family was in the neighborhood. On Christmas morning, "Santa" and his elves showed up on two white Jeep Cherokees and filled our entire living room with clothes, roller-blades, books, baseball bats and gloves for us kids, and kitchenware for my mother. It was the first time in my life that I saw my dad cry.

I remembered Christmas when I was twenty-four years old. My older brother, Andrey, organized a hundred people from our community to bring cards to elderly people spending Christmas without family. At one point in the evening, a few of us entered the room of a bedridden old man who could not join the cafeteria festivities. When we explained why we were there, he grabbed onto us, crying, and wouldn't stop thanking us for not passing by his room.

The man with the burned face sang, and I tried to keep the tears from rolling, clutching my Styrofoam coffee cup so tightly I was sure it would cave in. But when I glanced over at Carl next to me and saw him wiping his eyes with his handkerchief, I couldn't hold back any longer. I silently sobbed as the Christmas Eve service continued and didn't remember anything else that was sung or spoken for the remainder of the evening.

Carl and I walked back to the station in the way we had come, with his hand gripped tightly around my elbow, but this time we seemed to have no trouble in the snow. I felt like somebody had lifted a stone from my chest—I might as well have been floating over the snow. Preoccupied with our own musings, neither of us said a word.

I walked him to his sleeper and then found my own. I shut the light off and leaned back in my seat with my feet against the window, watching the snow swirl to the will of the wind. I remained that way until I fell asleep.

Nine

"When your feet are planted on solid ground, the sky is the limit."

It's impossible to understand how capable you truly are if you forget what you are made of. It seems that we all have long-term memory for our mistakes and failures, but short-term memory when it comes to the moments that made us.

I had felt like my feet were on shaky ground. Over the last several years, I had been stretching myself, doing many things I hadn't done before. I was often speaking to audiences who were undoubtedly more seasoned than I, competing for contracts with speakers who were much more accomplished than I, and I had to constantly implement new business practices I never imagined I would need to market myself and my books. Sometimes I succeeded, and sometimes I fell flat on my face. I put together events no one attended, created online programs no one bought, and spent our savings on coaches who taught me nothing.

I hadn't been sure of myself for what felt like a very long time. When you're in your comfort zone, you can at least sleep in peace because, for the most part, you are safe. There are very few surprises or moments of uncertainty. You're not putting anything on the line. But when expanding your mind and dreams, you're going to eat crap every once in a while. You'll get embarrassed, you'll lose money, you'll lose sleep, and you'll have to start all over. It is very humbling.

I knew it was necessary. I knew it meant I was growing. They say successful people fail fast and fail often, but I had been taking a lot of losses and had forgotten all about where I came from and what made me who I am. My faith in God, my family, and our humble beginnings, these were all things that made up the very fabric of my being.

How could I fail if I remembered that I came from grandparents who survived World War II, survived Hitler's concentration camps, and still lived lives that impacted thousands?

How could I fail if I remembered that I came from parents who left the Soviet Union with nothing but hope for the future and seven screaming kids under their arms? They came to America, trusting their children would have the opportunity to make something of themselves. They did this without understanding the language or having a spare dollar in their pockets.

How could I fail if I remembered the creator of the universe had permitted me to dream? *That* was solid ground. When I stood on that truth, I couldn't be stopped by rejection, criticism, competition, or my own fears. My dreams were bigger than my opposition; I just needed to remember that.

A tree can't grow tall without deep roots, a rocket can't launch into space from uneven ground, and a person can't achieve great things if they do not first have their feet steadied on a firm foundation. That evening at the church in Whitefish, I felt as if God Himself picked me up by the collar and set me on solid ground. I remembered who stood behind me. *When your feet are planted on solid ground, the sky is the limit.* Now I remembered.

***

"Merry Christmas, young man!" Oren bellowed as I stepped out of my sleeper. I woke up in the exact position I had fallen asleep in—legs crossed one over the other, knees locked with no support under them, and feet up against the window. It took a half hour of rubbing to reduce the painful stiffness, especially in the right knee, where I had reconstructive surgery after a football injury.

I don't remember the last time this had happened. I'd slept an entire night without so much as turning my head to one side or the other. Typically, that'd be the kind of thing that would wake me, and I'd be up the rest of the night. A testament to the peace that had come over me since the church experience last night, I concluded.

"Merry Christmas to you, Oren," I smiled. "Any chance you know when we might be leaving?"

"Yes, sir! The tracks have been cleared of the avalanche, and we'll be leaving within the hour! You should have received an alert on your phone," he pointed at my pocket.

I looked at my phone and saw the Amtrak notification requiring all passengers to be on board by 9:00 a.m.

"That's great, thank you," I said. I stopped by the bar, purchased a large coffee, and headed for the cabin at the end of the train after dumping some sugar and cream into my cup. A few frustrated passengers milled around the observation cars. I overheard two ladies complaining about missing Christmas morning with their families. While I understood their disappointment, I couldn't imagine a better vibe at that moment. "Grandma Got Ran Over by a Reindeer" played over the speaker system in the bar, two feet of fresh snow glimmered in the sun, and the charming little town set against the jagged peaks of the Rocky Mountains reminded me of one of those thousand-piece Thomas Kinkade puzzles. The gentle, steady hum of the train engine in the background only added to the soothing mood.

The only thing missing at that moment was my wife, family, and friends. Next year, I would see if I could convince an entire group to make this same trip on Christmas Eve. Especially since next year, I wouldn't be trying to escape everyone. Maybe I could even convince Carl to meet us in Whitefish. Nothing would make me happier than to introduce my new friend to Makenzie. She would adore him.

I was cozied up in my sweater, gripping my coffee, and staring out the window when Oren walked into the cabin, forehead scrunched and an uneasy look in his eyes.

"Michael, have you seen Carl this morning?" I was surprised he knew my name since I hadn't mentioned it to him the night before but realized he would have our sleeper car registrations available to him.

"No, sir, I haven't seen him or Austin since last night. I walked him to his room when we returned to the train." Oren's concern worried me a little. Austin entered the cabin just then, and we both looked expectantly at the kid. He hadn't seen Carl either.

"We are set to leave promptly, and I have not seen him since he stepped out early this morning, around 6:00 a.m." Oren looked at the digital tablet in his arm and flicked the screen up and down quickly, scrolling through what appeared to be a list of names. "And I don't believe we have a phone number registered for alerts under his reservation."

I suddenly realized Oren's concern was more urgent than my own. I was worried about Carl trying to get through the snow without my help, but Oren knew that Carl had not received the alert for the updated train schedule. The old man would not know the train would depart within the hour.

I set my coffee on the bar and headed for the exit with Austin right behind me. I didn't think to grab my coat, and as soon as we had made it a few blocks into town, the bitter Montana air penetrated my thin sweater. I was soon shivering uncontrollably, flashing back to something I'd read about how even cows regularly die in Montana winters. Austin and I peeked into coffee shop windows and restaurants, which were surprisingly open and quite busy with old folks on Christmas morning. Finding Carl in this crowd wouldn't be easy.

Several times I followed a WWII Veterans hat only to startle the poor, confused man I thought was Carl. As we progressed down Central Avenue, I shivered and breathed into my cupped fists to warm my hands.

"I sure as hell hope he's alright," Austin huffed and puffed behind me as we hurried down the sidewalk. I didn't reply. I hoped we'd missed Carl, and he was peacefully enjoying a cup of coffee back on the warm train. I realized now that I never asked the old man where he was headed in all the time we spent together these last twenty-four hours or so. But wherever it was, he wouldn't be arriving at his destination if we didn't find him soon.

Carl was an intelligent man, so I wasn't worried about him being lost or hurt. His mind was all there—it wasn't like we were looking for a lost dementia patient, far from it. In fact, there was something about Carl that I hadn't thought about before that moment.

I did the math, and Carl had to have been at least ninety-five years old, perhaps even older. But not only was he entirely there mentally, he was energetic, witty, and certainly very wise, and he also had been genuinely interested in Austin and me the previous evening. He listened, pried a little, and got us both talking about our lives as if we had known him forever, although he was very subtle about it. His curiosity about two complete strangers was surprising coming from a vet like him, especially one who was nearly a century old. Last night, I had figured it was the whiskey that greased us up. Now I wasn't so sure.

The old man had a presence about him that drew us in. It's probably why Oren was so worried back at the train and why the kid and I were slipping and sliding in our wet sneakers throughout town, searching for him. He had us all anxious.

Then I thought of something. "Follow me," I said to

Austin and headed for the church.

"Where else would I be besides where I must be on Christmas morning?" Carl chuckled as if he'd expected me to find him there and wasn't impressed by how long it took me to do it.

He wore an apron over his black windbreaker with the sleeves rolled up and reached down into a massive pot with the longest ladle I had ever seen, bringing it back up to pour steaming soup into one bowl after the other.

I had spotted his black cap with the gold embroidery as soon as we entered the church; he was the only one behind the serving cart not wearing a Santa hat. It was like finding Waldo in a crowded room, except every other volunteer was Waldo, and he was the only normal one. The old man was standing shoulder to shoulder with several servers. They all wore matching red aprons, and as the line of people with trays formed near the portable serving cart on wheels, they topped each tray with a biscuit, a thick slice of ham, mashed potatoes, and gravy, and a cup of juice. Then Carl placed a bowl of soup and a packet of crackers on each tray.

I couldn't believe that a small, freezing town like Whitefish had many homeless people. But as I looked down the line, I noticed that most people in line didn't appear to be homeless—there was a few rough-looking men but also mothers with children and tons of old folks. The line was made up of regular ordinary people in need.

"Most of these people wouldn't have a hot meal like this on Christmas morning . . . the church is doing what it was created to do and is serving them." Carl winked at me.

I would have loved to jump in and help any other day, but we were about to be left behind.

Ten

"When your heart breaks for those less fortunate than you, you can be entrusted with diamonds"

I must have checked my phone a hundred times as Austin and I waited for the line to clear. I had squeezed in between people to plead with Carl, hoping to convey the urgency of the situation, but he kept carefully filling bowls.

"I'll speak to you just as soon as everyone has been served," he had finally addressed me.

Every time a small child approached the cart with their tray, he took extra time to crack a joke or play a trick with his spoon to make them laugh before filling their bowls. I could hear the giggles from where Austin and I stood.

***

After a chaotic walk-run through the snow and thanks to some stalling by Oren, we were safely back on the train. I knew that if it had been any other passenger besides Carl, the train would have been halfway to West Glacier by now. Instead, Oren somehow managed to convince the engineer that leaving an American hero stranded in an unfamiliar town on Christmas would be the worst thing since the war itself. The three of us received plenty of dirty looks from passengers, now frustrated by another delay, but I couldn't care less. The old man was back on the train and that's all that mattered. He had undoubtedly tested our patience.

The train was back on the move, leaving the Whitefish station somewhere behind the magnificent snow-covered mountains. I brought an extra cup of coffee to help warm the old man and met him back at what we now called "our cabin."

"Oh . . . it's going to take a hell-of-a-lot more than some cold to take me out!" Carl insisted when Austin and I continued to check in with him to see if he was okay.

"When your heart breaks for those less fortunate than you, you can be entrusted with diamonds," The old man said with a sigh.

We settled into our usual seats, me on the couch with Austin and Carl across from us with shoes off, letting his socks dry. I sipped my coffee. I'd learned by now to be patient when he spoke. The more patient I was, the more gold came from his mouth. I didn't want to miss anything, so I shut up and waited.

After a few moments, Carl asked a question. "What does a person have to possess to be considered great . . . what would you two say that is?"

When he saw that Austin and I had no answer, he gave us a few options. "Is it wealth? Wisdom? Maybe fame? Or . . . maybe power?"

"All the above?" I guessed. I wasn't sure where he was going with his question.

Carl shook his head "No" and continued. "One day, Jesus' disciples argued amongst themselves and decided to ask Jesus about greatness. I don't know . . . I guess maybe they were feeling extra important that day and wanted some validation. But I don't believe he gave them the answer they wanted. Instead, he invited a little child to stand among them and said, 'Whoever humbles himself like this child is the greatest in the kingdom of heaven and whoever welcomes one such child in my name, welcomes me.'"

I saw Austin's eyebrows shoot up, "Wow! That's so good." he blurted. The kid was never short on enthusiasm.

"The disciples were hoping Jesus would elevate them

above everyone else." Carl continued. "They were hoping he would declare their greatness publicly. But instead of playing into their pride, he taught them that to be great; pride must be overcome by humility.

"Eventually, when they learned to become servants of the people, they became great. It's a good thing they were paying attention when Jesus was still around. Everyone wants to be important, do important things, and be recognized for it. People want to be entrusted with power, wealth, influence . . ." he said, stroking his beard. "But only those who are good stewards of such responsibility deserve the label of greatness."

Then the old man reached across and placed his hand on my knee.

"It doesn't take much character or integrity to earn a lot of money, become a leader, or to become a father. So you can't measure greatness by a man's title, bank account, or responsibility. But when a man's heart is set on defending the weak, and the fatherless, and the vulnerable and he becomes a servant of people . . . he is a man who can be entrusted with diamonds."

He then waved his cup from side to side as his eyes widened, hinting that Austin and I needed to pay extra attention to what he was about to say.

"Some say that money changes people, but money only *reveals* people. When you love others, especially those less fortunate, you can receive the world's riches, and they will not consume you. Your success will only enrich the lives of those around you as you adventure on in life. But if you only strive for success to elevate yourself above others . . . well, enjoy the downfall that will soon follow."

I looked down from his gaze—I could swear the old man was looking through my eyes and directly into my soul. I was uncomfortable. The way he spoke, with such conviction, I couldn't help but feel like his words were a blunt warning, and honestly, it scared me a bit. *That's quite the standard,* I thought. *Who the hell stands a chance of measuring up to that?* I didn't know if I could consider myself a servant to people or if it was even a priority for me anymore. I had a ton of personal ambitions. I wanted to be successful more than just about anything in the world. I wanted to prove to myself and everybody that I was no less capable than all the people out there already doing incredible things.

And after last night, I knew I was headed in the right direction. But maybe I was trying too hard to get into the spotlight. Maybe I was working to impact many but, at the same time, was neglecting the few that were already in my life.

I've heard it said this way, *Those who do not tend to the problems in their own home should not go about trying to fix the world.*

What were my motives? What if I only impacted one or two people?

Would I be fulfilled? Or was I only trying to earn recognition, to prove to everyone that I am somebody?

I wasn't sure, but I hated how those questions made me feel. I knew it was time, to be honest with myself.

I thought back to that little church in Whitefish, to that scar-faced singer, and to the old man in a little red apron filling the trays of little children. I wasn't even taking great care of the people I had already been entrusted with because I was so preoccupied with growing my influence. Fame and influence could help me sell more books and get me on more stages, but they certainly wouldn't bring me purpose if I missed the whole point.

The old man looked to the side for a moment, and suddenly his face turned to disgust.

"Just look at those TV and movie stars . . . look how many destroy themselves from the inside out with booze, drugs, and meaningless sex. They have influence and money coming out of their ass. Instead of being a conduit for good, they become like a sewage pipe, funneling nothing but crap into society and worse yet, teaching an entire generation of kids to be brainless and confused."

"You two young fellas have big dreams. You are working very hard, you are taking action, and I can tell you are persistent. Success and influence will surely follow. But may God have mercy on you if you don't learn now how to carry that responsibility with integrity and love for the *little children.* As Jesus once said, *'Whoever causes one of these little ones to stumble, it would be better for him if a millstone were hung around his neck and he were cast into the sea.'*"

I felt goosebumps on my arms from Carl's intense stare.

"Today, you did not only see little children in line at the church, right?" He did not wait for our response.

"You saw grown men and women desperate for community, to be loved and appreciated, just to be noticed for once. Are they also not only little children in the eyes of God? That is exactly what they are!" He exclaimed.

He paused for a moment, and his face relaxed.

"No matter how important you become, they *are* your responsibility. And it starts at home. Become a servant of people, and you will be great! Then you can be entrusted with diamonds!"

***

We covered new terrain every minute as the tracks carved through jagged mountains, creeks, fields, and forests, taking us across snowy bridges and pitch-black tunnels. I couldn't help but think about the poor chaps who laid the railroad through this rugged "God's Country." I decided then and there this was a trip I would make annually. Whether it was with company or on my own, I couldn't get enough of these vistas.

I looked over at Austin, who had both elbows on his knees and hands clasped together as he listened to Carl.

I don't know if I would be too concerned with the well-being of others if my child were undergoing cancer treatment. Of course, I understood Carl was making a point about leadership, carrying one's responsibility with integrity, and being entrusted with influence and success. Still, I just didn't know how I would have lived had I been forced to trade places with the kid.

Maybe Austin is a much better man than I could ever be, I thought. It's easy to understand life's principles in theory; it becomes a different story when life punches you in the face and dares you not to crumble.

I have a one-dimensional outlook when it comes to family. It's family over everything else for me—over personal goals and desires, over personal health and safety, over personal happiness and peace. I would go to hell and back for any of my siblings. But I couldn't begin to imagine the darkness one had to endure for their child.

I admired the way Austin carried himself despite his burden. Some people are physically strong, and some are strong in the things that really matter—the mind and the spirit.

There wasn't a hint of victimhood or blame in the kid, and despite all the troubles already stacked against him in his young life, he still managed to make others feel noticed, heard, and understood. It was an exceptional quality. I could learn a thing or two from someone like Austin.

He was a man who could be entrusted with diamonds.

Eleven

"Life is happening with or without you"

After I had finished my third cup of coffee, I pushed myself up from the couch. "Well, I think it's time for some lunch," I stood, stretched, and was about to head for the cabin door when Carl grabbed my arm.

"Just a moment, Michael," he said in a low voice while his eyes followed Austin. Austin stood and walked to the door, then turned to face us.

"I think I'll have a bite to eat as well. I'm sure I'll see you guys here in a bit." He waved his hand, turned, and stepped out of the cabin.

"Yep!" I yelled after him.

Still seated with his cane across his lap, Carl clasped my palm into his leathery hands and squeezed as he spoke. "You never know what war rages behind a smiling man's face," he whispered gently.

Suddenly, his face seemed sad, as if he was foreseeing something he could not express with words. His bushy white brows scrunched together, and the corners of his mouth drooped. I thought something had gone wrong, or perhaps the old man was dreading wherever he was headed. Or maybe he wasn't feeling well.

But before I could ask, he squeezed my hands tighter still.

"Life is happening with or without you." He spoke carefully and glanced at the door where Austin had been seconds before.

"The kid is having a harder time than he is showing. I can see it in his eyes. He's hanging on by a thread, dear boy. Don't you miss this moment. Now is all you have. Today is the day to lift someone."

Tears formed in the old man's eyes. I immediately felt a lump growing in my throat. I couldn't understand why he was speaking as if this was the last time we would see each other. I wanted to remind him that I was just going to grab some lunch and would be back, that we still had at least another day together, but I was getting the feeling that this was the end.

The wrinkled skin on his cheeks was wet now, and he still clutched my hands. I squeezed back tightly, letting him know he had my attention.

"This life, all the troubles and the fears, all the pain, and the tears, all the terrible things people say and all the nasty things they will do to each other—this will all pass away faster than you think. No one will remember your mistakes and failures because no one is even thinking about you; they are thinking about themselves.

"Your self-doubts are like a bag of junk slung over your shoulder. And you are clinging to them as if somehow bringing them along with you everywhere you go will help you sort them out. But my ambitious friend, they're only weighing you down. So stop carrying them. Leave the baggage on this train when you get home. No more. You'll never get to where you want to go by accident, and you'll especially never do it if you are weighed down."

He tried to smile and dropped my hands to wipe his eyes with a handkerchief before continuing. "Unfortunately, in the end, no one besides God will understand your journey and what battles you fought when the nights were the darkest. History doesn't judge us by our intentions, only our actions, only the results. Just go and be great!"

The old man poked a bony finger into my chest, "You were searching for answers and chose to jump on this train, and because of it, you made new friends and had new conversations. But you could have just as easily decided to stay home under your little cloud of fear and self-pity, and everything would have stayed the same.

"Life is nothing but a series of choices. If you are open, willing, and hungry and choose to jump on the opportunities presented, you will be used in incredible ways. You will become a conduit God can work through to touch the lives of those who need to be touched."

After a moment's pause, Carl squeezed my forearm. "If you choose to downplay your abilities, turn a blind eye to opportunities, and keep questioning whether or not you are headed in the right direction, you will miss it. Again my friend . . . life is happening with or without you."

I ate alone in my roomette. I could not get the old man's words out of my head. I kept picturing his wrinkled face and pleading brown eyes. I couldn't understand the desperation. I didn't know why he was suddenly so concerned about the kid. Why was he insisting that I not miss this particular moment? Had Austin said something to Carl that made him so distraught?

The old man knew something I didn't.

***

I woke from a deep sleep when the train came to a complete stop. I had somehow drifted into one of those daytime naps where you have to sit and stare at your surroundings for a few minutes when you wake up before your brain finally comprehends what year it is and where the heck you are. After I was convinced that I was now back to reality, I pulled the curtains aside and peeked out the window.

The station wasn't much to look at. The old building resembled a big chicken coop, and if it weren't for the big brown letters nailed to the side of the building announcing SHELBY, I wouldn't have guessed it was a routine stop.

I brushed my teeth and pulled my sneakers on. Instead of tying the laces, I shoved them into the shoe to keep them from flailing loosely and stepped out of my cabin.

When I walked into the last car, I immediately noticed the empty shelves behind the bar of the first cabin. Weird. *Oren must have cleared the shelves this morning,* I guessed. Though I wondered why he would have gone through all the trouble of stocking and removing the liquor so suddenly—and on our second day of the trip.

The two cabins were empty, so I turned to leave, but before I stepped out, I spotted a slight tear on the green velvet of one of the barstools. I ran my fingers over it. To my surprise, it looked like it might have developed over years of use, not something that was recently torn. I knew it to be an antique car but guessed I hadn't noticed the wear until now. Then I looked down at my feet. Oddly enough, the bottle green carpet, which had been fluffy and spotless, now looked worn and stained down the middle of the cabin by foot traffic over the years.

I left the cabin and walked back up the train. When I approached Carl's sleeper room, it, too, was empty. The blanket was neatly folded on top of the pillow, just as it had been in my room at the beginning of the trip. The pillow was still wrapped in the clear plastic covering with an Amtrak's Cleanliness Guarantee sticker and looked like it hadn't been touched.

Confused, I took a step back and counted the rooms, ensuring I was standing at the door I had walked him to the previous evening. This was definitely the right room. Perhaps Carl hadn't used the blanket and pillow provided for him. I wouldn't be surprised; the old vet probably didn't want to make extra laundry for the Amtrak staff. My dad is like that—he never uses the fancy napkins in restaurants because he doesn't want them to be "ruined." I couldn't blame those generations. They came from different times, hard times.

As I was still standing in front of Carl's spotless sleeper, Oren walked into the car. I smiled, "Hey, Oren! It looks like Carl packed up and left the train early."

"I'm sorry?" Oren looked puzzled like he didn't get my joke.

"Looks like Carl packed up and left the train early," I repeated, smiling as I pointed into the room.

Oren's face remained emotionless.

"Do you know your room number, sir?" he asked me

politely. I was taken aback, partially because Oren didn't match my friendliness as I expected and partly because he acted like he had never seen me before and had forgotten my name.

Maybe he's busy and isn't in the mood right now. Or perhaps he got into trouble for our delay earlier that morning and isn't too happy with me.

"Yes," I replied quickly, "my room is in a different car. I didn't see Carl in the cabin at the end of the train, so I figured he was back in his room."

Oren looked into Carl's room and eyed me suspiciously. "Sir, we try to ensure all of our travelers feel safe and comfortable for the entirety of their trip. If your room is not in this car, I would appreciate it if you headed back to your car. Unless, of course, you would like to use the observation or bar cars. You are more than welcome to wander in that area as you please. Thank you."

Oren walked away in a hurry, looking down at the tablet in his arm. My feet were frozen to the floor. I was stunned at how the jolly conductor had transformed into a rude, humorless pencil-pusher who was now not-so-kindly warning me to stop *wandering* around where I did not belong.

Embarrassed, I slowly made my way back to an observation car and sat in one of two empty recliners facing the windows. If I hadn't been caught off guard, I would have fired something back at Oren. Instead, I found myself slumped in the seat, trying to replay in my head all that had transpired in the last couple of hours since I had left the cabin at the end of the train for lunch.

What the hell was Oren's problem? And where was Carl?

Just as I was about to get up and walk the train again to see if perhaps I had missed the old man in my earlier pass-through, Austin dropped into the seat next to me.

"Austin!" I just about yelled. "Have you seen Carl?"

The kid had just put his face into his hands and jerked his head violently to look up at me when he heard his name. "I'm . . . I'm not sure . . . who Carl is?" he stuttered and swallowed nervously. His eyes were swollen, and I could tell he had been crying, but I pressed on. I had questions.

"You're messing with me, right!?" I lowered my voice, but my tone did not change. "We were just with him a few hours ago . . . you, and Carl! And Oren was just a prick to me. What's up with him?"

The kid's confused stare didn't convince me, so I continued, "Come on, man, you're messing with me. Carl's a pretty unforgettable guy, especially after that freezing man-hunt through the snow he made us go on this morning . . . have you seen him since we left him in the cabin?"

"I'm sorry, sir, I don't know who you're talking about.

127

I'm traveling alone. Maybe I look like someone you know?" The kid's face turned from confusion to concern, and my head spun.

Had I completely lost my mind or were these guys pulling some prank on me? I would have demanded Austin come clean with the gag, but he didn't look like someone interested in playing along with a joke at that moment. And the way Oren treated me, something was wrong. "It's that damn nap," I said under my breath. *Maybe I should go back to sleep, and everything will be normal again when I wake up. What the heck is happening?*

"Your . . . your name is Austin, right?" I looked right into his eyes. I knew it was. Why was I even asking him? Of course, his name was Austin! We spent the entire trip together!

"Yes," he replied, startled, "I'm sorry if I don't remember where we met. I've had a rough couple of days recently." He attempted a smile and reached out his hand.

"Oh, don't worry about it," I mumbled as I shook his hand.

I wanted to question him, just for my own sanity's sake, just to convince myself I hadn't somehow made the entire last day and half of the events up in my mind. But when I looked in the kid's eyes, I couldn't bring myself to ask him if he had a little girl who was recently diagnosed with cancer.

Twelve

"Allow yourself to be moved emotionally"

I tried to calm my voice even though my thoughts were running on overdrive and my heart was thumping in my chest something fierce. As hard as I tried to remember the sequence of events that led to this moment, I could not piece it all together.

I met great men yesterday, we had incredible life-changing conversations and moments, and then I woke up from a nap, and suddenly one of them apparently doesn't exist, and the other doesn't even remember my name?

I turned to the kid and softly asked the question. "Austin, I don't mean to stick my nose in your business, but is everything alright with you?"

He stared at the floor. He didn't seem agitated by my question, and I was relieved. I exhaled slowly through my nose and waited. *Will he confirm what I already know about his life? I couldn't have imagined all that had happened. I know his name; doesn't that prove I didn't make this entire thing up?*

"I'm a complete failure, sir," he said and began to cry. He stuck his face back into his hands, and his shoulders shook as he sobbed. "My little girl is sick," he stammered in between ragged breaths. "My career is a bust, and worst of all . . . I'm coming home broke and empty-handed on Christmas. Pathetic!"

I shook my head from side to side and put my hand on his back. He was hunched over, leaning on his knees. I wanted so badly to ask him if he really didn't remember me. Or better yet, why was he lying and pretending not to recognize me?

Austin and Oren were either great pranksters that Carl had put up to this, or I had just snapped out of some trance or dream. And yet, I knew it couldn't have *all* been an illusion—I knew private details about the kid's life that he had just confirmed!

I knew his little girl was sick . . . very sick, I knew he wasn't doing well as a salesman, I knew he was coming home to Chicago after a failed trip selling roofs in the Pacific Northwest. Just to make sure, I waited a moment and turned to him.

"Austin, you sell roofs, right?"

The kid raised his head, straightened his back, and looked at me, baffled. I continued, almost whispering my following two questions, "And you were just in

Washington for a few weeks leading up to the holidays trying to make a few sales . . . and your little girl has cancer?" I swallowed hard and pulled my hand away so he wouldn't feel it trembling.

He looked behind me, then around the entire observation car, then into my eyes. "Yes," he whispered. "How did . . ."

I interrupted him. "I don't know how I know that," I lied. If this kid honestly didn't remember me, I wasn't about to explain that I had just spent the last twenty-four hours making imaginary friends with him, the conductor, and some old World War II veteran who happened to be incredibly fond of him.

Just then, I saw Oren walking down the aisle of the observation car.

"Sir!" I called to him and raised my hand. He looked annoyed when he saw it was me, the guy who had been creeping around people's cabins.

"Can you tell me what the next stop is?" I waited as he quickly scrolled through his tablet.

"Next stop is Havre, Montana," he said abruptly.

"And will there be a returning train passing through Havre anytime soon? Something has come up, and I must get home immediately."

Oren took a deep breath and exhaled, visibly bothered

that I was wasting his time once again. He leaned on the back of a seat cushion, crossed his feet, and began tapping away at the tablet. I waited patiently. Several times I glanced between Oren and Austin, curious to see if the two showed any familiarity, but they never once acknowledged each other.

The chubby conductor seemed to be reluctant to give me good news. "Looks like there is. You will have to wait three hours at the station in Havre for the returning line to come through. If you are fine with that, I can make that transfer happen now." He waited for my response without looking up at me.

This jerk was nothing like the friendly Oren I met earlier . . . in my dream, or trance, or vision, or whatever the heck it was.

"Yes, sir, please do. Thank you." I stood and stretched out my hand to him. He was surprised by my gesture and quickly moved his tablet to his left arm to shake my hand. I held his hand for a moment and looked him in the eyes. Even though he had been rude, I knew who he really was deep down. I knew he was a kind, jolly man who loved his job. Perhaps he, too, was having a rough few days.

I smiled and spoke to the man I remembered him to be, not the man he had been this last hour or so. "Thank you so much for your care and hospitality on this trip. It has been a life-changing ride. I'll never forget it." I gently slapped his shoulder with my other hand and finally let go of his grip.

Oren's demeanor changed immediately. He dropped his shoulders, and his expression softened. I turned and sat back down next to Austin. Out of the corner of my eye, I saw the conductor look back at me as he walked away.

I smiled to myself. Whether Carl was real or not, I remembered his words and I would never again miss an opportunity to encourage someone.

I didn't know what had happened. And I didn't understand why it happened to me here, on this trip I took to get away from people, not become involved in their lives. But I knew my friend Carl, whoever and wherever he was, had changed my life.

***

Austin wanted to know how I knew so much about him, but I stood up. "Want to see something cool?" I asked.

He shrugged his shoulders and adjusted his glasses like I had seen him do on this trip at least a hundred times. I waved for him to follow me. We stopped by the bar car to order two double Old-Fashioneds and carefully proceeded to the cabin at the end of the train.

I watched Austin admire the antique cabin, much like he had done the first time I met him though it certainly showed its age this time. "Pretty neat, huh?" I smiled. I took a seat where I had sat the entire trip, and he sat across from me, in Carl's favorite spot. A small chunk of foam padding was bulging from a tear in the couch.

"That definitely wasn't there before," I muttered.

"Allow yourself to be moved emotionally." I heard the words in my head as if someone had whispered them into my ear. I knew what those words meant. I knew that emotion was the life-blood of motivation. I knew that a person could set any big goal they wanted for themselves, but if they weren't somehow emotionally attached to that goal, they could try with all their might but never achieve it. Emotion drives us. Whether it's anger, hate, fear, passion, or love—we act on the things that make us *feel* something.

I understood that.

But I had been so focused on progressing forward that I left no time and space in my routine to *feel* anything. Everything had become automatic: a list of daily tasks that formed a pattern that eventually created my habits and controlled my state of mind. My dream had become all process and no passion, results-driven, but running increasingly low on heart and soul.

I needed to allow myself to be touched and moved again

by conversations, and experiences, and people, just as much as failures, and distractions, and disappointments moved me. I had become numb to the troubles others were experiencing. Living in my head for so long had made me indifferent to the world around me. Before this trip, I had to admit there was very little that stirred up any emotion in me anymore.

I used to be easily inspired, moved, and touched by simple things. An old Russian war song would make me cry. I couldn't retell specific stories from my childhood without choking up. I'd see a musician perform in a bar and consider them the best musician I'd ever heard. I made friends easily, and I opened up to them quickly. My surroundings heavily influenced me, and I was grateful just to be alive. It had always been one of my greatest strengths, my ability to appreciate and be moved by the little things in life. I think I learned it from my mom and dad.

I wanted that back. If I wanted to be at peace, to be alive, to be present, I had to become sensitive to life happening all around me again. How many moments had I missed simply because I was so deep in my little world?

I thought about all the times my little nieces and nephews did something new for the first time, but I didn't stop to celebrate. All the strangers that displayed kindness to one another in public, but I only noticed the hate and division spread by the news. I wondered if there were times when perhaps, at the grocery store, I had made eye contact with someone on their last day on earth, but I didn't give them a smile.

I immediately remembered the man in overalls at the coffee shop only a few days ago. I wished now I hadn't turned a cold shoulder to his friendliness. Why couldn't I have just given him even twenty seconds of my attention?

I had become hardened and insensitive.

With Carl's help, I knew I could get that back. I remembered how liberated I felt last night after the Christmas service in Whitefish.

Yes, that *is the power of allowing myself to be moved emotionally.*

I glanced at my phone and saw an Amtrak notification had appeared. We would be arriving in Havre in a few minutes. I stood, stepped across the worn carpet to where Austin was seated, and stretched my hand to him. He shook it.

"Austin," I said, looking directly into his blue eyes. "One day, you will impact millions of people with your life. You are stronger than you know and more capable than you can ever imagine. You can handle anything life throws at you and your family; I can see it in your eyes. When you get back to Chicago, you hug that little girl of yours, and you believe for her healing . . . and then on Monday morning, you call your guy, and you tell him you'll take that position, even if it does scare the hell out of you to speak in front of large groups of people."

Austin looked at me, mouth agape. Tears appeared in his eyes. I didn't wait for a response. I stepped out of the cabin just as the train slowed down at Havre station.

***

I watched the mountains from in my new sleeper room on the train, now headed in the opposite direction, towards home, and prayed. "God, I'm only a blip on the timeline of your history books . . . I won't pretend that my life is somehow your gift to the universe, but it is your gift to me. I understand that now more than ever. With the time you have given me, I will do everything in my power to do my part in this world. And I'll never let my little bubble of fears, insecurities, and worries ever hinder my gift again."

In these miraculous thirty-two hours since I'd stepped onto the train in Vancouver, I had reconnected with my purpose. I had been reminded that *sometimes the things we run from are the very things we should be moving towards,* that *our eyes are the window through which the soul sees the world,* that *sometimes we will feel afraid and unqualified, and that was okay,* that along the way, *we will be pulled in all directions.*

I knew that when times get tough, *all we needed was a little perspective,* that we *couldn't wait to be discovered,* and if we really wanted something, we could *believe it into existence.*

I remembered that *faith without action is dead because action activates miracles,* that *when our feet are planted on solid ground, the sky is the limit for us,* that *when our heart breaks for those less fortunate than us, we can be entrusted with diamonds.* I understood that *life is happening with or without us,* and it was up to us to live with intention.

But most importantly, I realized that there are people all around me in this world hanging on to their lives by a thread, and if I didn't *allow myself to be moved emotionally,* I would miss it all. It is up to me to live according to my talents, gifts, and abilities so that I might be in a position to throw out a life preserver when needed.

If not me, then who!?

For Og Mandino, it was Napoleon Hill. For me, it was Og Mandino and Carl Talbot. And who knows, it might be me for some poor soul out there. It might be you.

I kept it together as I carried my bag across the parking lot to where Makenzie was parked, but when I climbed into the car and kissed her, I fell apart. She stared at me with a terrified look on her beautiful thin face. Her eyes were wide, thinking something horrible must have happened. As I reassured her I was fine, I couldn't keep the tears from coming.

She was another reminder of all I had taken for granted in life.

I knew I had tough days ahead in the pursuit of my dreams. I knew there would be moments when I felt frightened, unqualified, and full of self-doubt. But as my wife drove our car away from the station, I knew exactly where I was headed and who I needed to be.

At home, I switched on the light on my desk in my office, slumped into my chair, and stared at the ceiling for an hour. I thought about the cabin at the end of the train, the church in Whitefish, the old man, and then about Austin.

Then something in my backpack caught my eye. I had tossed my bag in the corner of my office, and the main pocket's zipper was slightly open. I noticed the familiar golden embroidery. I pulled the bag open and reached inside. When I pulled out the faded black hat, my heart leaped in my chest.

It had to have been Carl's. *I hadn't imagined the old man after all!* I peered inside the lining of the hat and spotted some scribbling in black Sharpie.

CARL W. TALBOT

20th ARMORED DIVISION.

I walked back to my desk, flipped open my laptop, typed

20th ARMORED DIVISION into the search bar, and read the results aloud.

"On April 29, 1945, the 20th Armored Division was one of three US Army divisions to take part in the liberation of the Dachau concentration camp."

I pushed my chair back from my desk and laughed, "You've got to be kidding me!"

"What's going on?" Makenzie called from the other room.

"Oh . . . it's nothing," I replied.

Carl and his boys had saved my grandpa.

The End

About the Author

Michael was born in Soviet Russia, came to the United States just before the end of the Cold War as a political refugee, and is the grandson of a Siege of Leningrad and Dachau camp survivor. Today, Michael is a Game-Changing motivational speaker and Best-Selling author who has impacted thousands of people with his message of resilience, purpose, and hope. He is on a mission to help people discover a better way to live.

If you would like to have Michael speak at your corporate event, school, retreat, church, or any other event, please visit Michael's website here:

WWW.SPEAKLIFE365.COM

Acknowledgments

Editor:
Madeleine Eno, as always, THANK YOU for your work on this book!

Illustrator:
Jesse Hostetler, thank you for the cover design!

Be sure to find Michael's other books:

The Mount of Olives:
11 Declarations to an Extraordinary Life

Combining courage, faith, wisdom and wonder into an inspiring tale of self-discovery, The Mount of Olives takes readers for an emotional ride through the life of a boy whose search for better becomes a discovery of something extraordinary. Michael Ivanov's masterpiece tells the story of Felix, the Roman boy who despite all opposition, yearns to gain a worldly treasure. His journey will lead him to riches far different—and far more satisfying—than he ever imagined. Felix's quest teaches us the essential wisdom of listening to our hearts, recognizing opportunity and learning the golden principles strewn along life's path, and, most importantly, to follow our dreams.

The Traveler's Secret:
Ancient Proverbs for Better Living

The Traveler's Secret offers an ancient story of one man's choices—and the principles that make the difference between failure and success. In this fable about following dreams, Michael V. Ivanov's latest masterpiece reveals the journey of Agisillus, a vagabond in ancient Gaul, and his extraordinary encounter with a mysterious traveler. This book reveals secrets to living an extraordinary and purposeful life, amassing personal wealth, and leaving a legacy that continues to sow seeds of life into the world. It shares the ancient proverbs of the wise and the foolish and teaches the universal laws of prosperity. Author Michael V. Ivanov provides concrete advice for living a wise and purposeful life.

The four scrolls:

Scroll 1 The Cultivation

Scroll 2 The Burial

Scroll 3 The Resurrection

Scroll 4 The Harvest.

The Servant With One Talent:
Five Success Principles from the Greatest Parable Ever Told

To bring your dreams and desires to fulfillment, you must invest in your talents. This book shows you how to become successful and live with purpose by sharing the secrets hidden in an ancient parable, which holds the universal laws of prosperity.

The Servant With One Talent is an instant classic that holds the key to all you desire and everything you wish to accomplish. Through the story of the unprofitable and lazy servant in ancient Babylon, Michael V. Ivanov provides a unique perspective on the classic parable of the talents. This book provides concrete advice for creating a successful and purposeful life while fulfilling your destiny and becoming the person you were created to be. While many people are burying their dreams, talents, skills and abilities in the desert, like the unprofitable servant did at the beginning of this story, the successful are investing into their skills, talents, and abilities.

The Five success principles in The Servant With One Talent:

1. To each, according to his abilities.
2. A talent buried is a talent lost.
3. Do not concern yourself with your neighbor's wages
4. The time is now.
5. To those who have, much more will be given, from those who have not, what little they have will be taken from them.

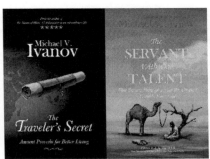

Get signed copies of all of Michael's books at
WWW.MOUNTOFOLIVESBOOK.COM

Made in the USA
Columbia, SC
09 November 2023

25845742R00093